QUEER LOVE

Queer Love

An Anthology of Irish Fiction

Edited by Paul McVeigh

SOUTHWORDeditions

First published in 2020
by Southword Editions
The Munster Literature Centre
Frank O'Connor House, 84 Douglas Street
Cork, Ireland

Set in Adobe Caslon 12pt

ISBN 978-1-905002-84-9

Second printing 2021

Ionad Munster
Litríochta Literature
an Deisceart Centre

the arts
council
chomhairle
ealaíon

funding
literature
artscouncil.ie

Comhairle Cathrach Chorcaí
Cork City Council

CONTENTS

FOREWORD

When I was a young boy I hid in the library. I was hiding
from a troubled home, from the troubled streets of Belfast,
but, mostly, from the kind of trouble being an effeminate
boy got you. I was more frightened of that constant abuse
and hatred than I was of bombs and bullets. I was safe in
the library. I was protected by books. I don't think this
is an uncommon scenario for us outsiders in our youth,
especially those of my generation. Perhaps the library
was the original 'safe space'. Without having been forced
there would I have developed my love of books? I think
so. Reading was a much needed escape but books also
brought knowledge, and, crucially, became the shields and
weapons I needed to survive the world outside.

As I got older, my world broadened, one book led to
another, and bigger libraries in town would help with
the label on the shelf announcing 'of interest' to me. I
couldn't bring these books home, but I spent hours from
school's end to closing time searching for stories of those
who lived my life before me.

I read to find out about other people and other worlds, real and imagined, sure, but I also read for the increasingly desperate need to discover I was not alone. I dreamed of my own escape, to find my tribe. These were pre-internet days, back when LGBTQI+ representation on TV and in film was rare. Stories about people like me weren't always easy to find. Irish ones even harder. Is that part of the reason that, in the past, so many of us left home, not just to be free of oppression but also because we saw ourselves represented on foreign shores?

Patrick Cotter of Southword Editions got in touch with me a few months ago as he had been reflecting on the 1996 Gill & MacMillan anthology *The Irish Eros* edited by David Marcus, which featured just two pieces acknowledging the existence of Irish gay life and one of those was a poem by a straight man. He wanted to produce an anthology that would seek to go some way to redress the lack of acknowledgement of the LGBTQI+ community in Irish literary anthologies in general. *Queer Love* is it.

We have a mixture of established writers of international standing, writers who have been making a splash in recent years, and new emerging writers. The anthology also has a mixture of previously published stories, newly commissioned work and those entered through our call out.

Is it a sign of the times that people seem focused on what something isn't as opposed to what it is? I've had people ask me why the book isn't longer, why it isn't an encyclopedic survey of Irish LGBTQI+ writers throughout history, why 'old' writers are included when it could showcase all new writers? I've been told it shouldn't even exist unless it can fulfil every quota and cover all concerns. *Queer Love*'s shoulders can only carry so much ambition. A great piece of writing advice I've read, I'll paraphrase: 'If you don't see the book you want to read then write it yourself'. I'd posit this to those who want this anthology to be different, fulfilling all of the above ideas and ideas yet unspoken. Provide more shields and weapons, maybe some comfort and loving arms too, a trail of breadcrumbs that lead to our tribes on home shores. Let's fill those bookshelves in homes, libraries, and shops with more and more stories of us.

—Paul McVeigh
November 2020

ARABY

BY JOHN BOYNE

North Richmond Street, my aunt told me, was a quiet street until I was sent to live there. Neither she nor my uncle had wanted me with them, I knew that much, but what choice did they have when my parents left for Canada, claiming that they would send for me when they were settled? My aunt showed me the box room that was once my cousin's and told me not to get too comfortable.

Jack's room was exactly as he left it on the day he wandered into the path of a number 7 bus as it made its way around Mountjoy Square towards the Rotunda Hospital. The toys and games were a little young for me, the books were ones I'd read a few years before, but I didn't mind for I felt a longing to wrap myself in the comfort of the past. I had lived in a big house before all the trouble started, when we had money, but that was gone now. People said it was my father's fault, or at least that he bore a considerable portion of the blame, and there were those who said he should be brought back from Canada to face the courts. They said he had destroyed lives and that families would not recover for generations. I scanned my uncle's copy of *The Irish Times* every morning in hope that they would achieve their goal; I wanted my father brought home. And my mother too, I suppose.

11

It was late autumn and the nights drew in early but I preferred to be outside than stuck within those suffocating walls. The house was stale, the wallpaper peeled in corners above the cooker revealing a yellow-mottled skin behind. There was a dog who was no fun and whoever heard of such a thing as that? My aunt sat in front of the television most of the day, drinking tea and eating custard cremes, a cigarette always on the go. My uncle, a civil servant, preferred the pub after five o'clock and I didn't blame him. Occasionally they spoke to each other. A school had not been organised for me yet; they said it would come soon but the days passed and no changes happened there. I didn't mind. I yearned for company but couldn't bear the idea of having to make new friends. Boys my age intimidated me; they always had. And to be a new boy at a new school? There were few ideas more alarming.

Some afternoons, I would wander up Ballybough Road and turn right towards Fairview Park, which was big enough for me to investigate in sections. I found empty bottles of cider, small black bags filled with dog shit, Sunday supplements, half-eaten sandwiches and once, a pair of women's underwear ripped asunder at the seam as if someone had removed them with violence. I saw a man crying on a bench as he read a letter, digging the nails of one hand into the palms of the other. I watched a boy and a girl kissing in a copse, his hand moving greedily beneath her shirt, and when he noticed me, the boy gave chase until I collapsed, panting on the damp grass, and let him slap me about the face a few times.

There was only one child living nearby, a girl of my age named Mangan, but it was her brother, a few years older than she who caught my eye and made me hope for a protector. He went to school in a uniform but came home most afternoons in rugby shorts, his face mud-striped and wild, the hairs on his legs clay-caked to his skin.

Every morning, I watched from my bedroom window as he left the house, yawning, his bag slung over his shoulder, his tie already loosened around his neck as he put the black buds in his ears, scrolled to the music he wanted and went on his way. Then I would charge down the stairs, out the door and run after him, glad that his music cocoon prevented him from hearing me marching along behind. If he turned he would see me, of course, but he never turned. And had he noticed me, I would have pretended not to see him at all but would have simply trotted along, ignoring him, a boy off on some piece of private business. I thought of him through the day and wondered whether he was taking notes in class, talking with his friends, changing for his match. I wondered what kind of sandwiches he ate at lunchtime and what he washed them down with.

He was on my mind constantly and it frightened me that I could think of no one else. Were boys not supposed to think of girls, had I not read that somewhere? He had thick, messy blonde hair that looked as if it never saw a comb and was stocky, like rugby players often are. How old was he, sixteen perhaps? Just a boy but a man from my perspective, a few years his junior. I saw him everywhere, both awake and asleep, and knew not why. I caught sight of him in a supermarket one afternoon, a girl walking along with him, and followed him through every aisle, my eyes on their hands, hoping their fingers would never connect. I wanted him to move away, or for my

13

parents to send for me, so that I might stop obsessing, but dreaded the notion of a *For Sale* sign going up across the street. I was as confused in my adoration as I was excited by it. I imagined what it would be like to be his friend, for him to hold me. He might hand one of his earpieces to me so we could listen to a song together, our faces close out of necessity. We would smile at each other, our bodies touching as our heads bounced in time with the music. He would reach for the earphone afterwards, his fingers grazing my cheek and smile at me.

The gap between his front teeth. The scratch of stubble along his chin. The coloured thread he wore around his wrist. His habit of wearing runners with his school trousers. All these things were matters that I took note of and thought about, day and night.

Once, when I woke too late to see him leave, I returned to my virgin bed in my dead cousin's room and threw myself around beneath the blanket, thrashing like a wild animal, my feet wrapping the pale sheets around my ankles, mummifying myself in their whiteness as I kicked out in self-loathing and buried my face in my pillow crying out his name, spoken with longing, then with vulgarities attached, then obscenities, until finally, spent and soiled, the sheets a disgrace, I examined my thin young body and felt as alone as I have ever felt in my life, the isolation of a boy who feels that an unfairness has been thrust upon him that he will never be able to share for who would ever understand such a thing or tell him that he is not a monster?

At last he spoke to me, asking why I never went to school. I told him there were plans in that direction but they seemed slow in coming to fruition.

'You're the lad with the father in the papers all the time, aren't you?' he asked and I nodded, embarrassed by my father's disgrace but flattered that I had some celebrity in his eyes. 'Do you play rugby at all?'

'Not yet,' I said. 'Maybe when I start school.'

'Do you watch it?'

'On the telly.'

'Sure come up some Saturday morning to the school and watch one of our matches. Half past eleven till just before one. Lots of lads your age do. Bring us an orange for afterwards,' he added, laughing before running across the road without even a goodbye and leaving me on the banks of the Tolka River, alone and delirious. I wanted him to take more care on the roads than my poor cousin had.

Saturday morning came and my aunt said I was to stay at home until she and my uncle were back from the shops as there was a delivery that they were waiting on.

'Can they not leave it next door?' I asked and she turned, annoyed by my refusal to help, and said that she didn't want to go bothering the neighbours.

'I don't ask much of you,' she snapped. 'What use are you anyway if you won't do one simple thing after we've given you a home and food and a bed to sleep in?'

Eleven o'clock came and no sign of the man from An Post. Eleven-thirty. Twelve. I could feel my stomach turning in convulsions and once, in a fit of dramatics, I convinced myself that I was going to be sick with anxiety and hung my head over the toilet bowl. I went outside and stared anxiously up and down the street in search of the van. I marched around the house, cursing all those who worked for the postal service and banged my fist off the bedroom wall until I thought it might bruise. Finally at twelve-thirty the doorbell rang, the parcel arrived and it needed no signature at all despite what my aunt had said and I threw it on the kitchen table in a fury, grabbing the freshest looking orange I could find from the fruit bowl and ran through the streets towards the school where the brother of the Mangan girl played his rugby.

I was afraid that the match would be over by the time I got there but no, a crowd of a hundred people or more were gathered on the side-lines on all four sides of the pitch, a sea of blue and white for one team and green and gold for the other. They were cheering the lads on and I looked out for Mangan, whose back bore the number nine, and followed him with my eyes.

A girl was standing next to me with two boys and I listened in to their conversation.

'That's what I heard anyway.'

'It's not true.'

'It is! I happened at the party last Friday.'

'I heard he was into your one from St Anne's.'

'It was her was into him.'

'That's a lie.'

The girl turned and looked down at me and asked me what I thought I was doing and I blushed and made my way down the field, watching as the ball was thrown from player to player, scrums were formed, lines were drawn, throw-ins were made and tries were scored. I saw the brother of the Mangan girl take the gum shield from his mouth during a break in play and watched the way his upper lip contorted as he released it, his tongue extending for a moment before diving back inside. A line of saliva ran like a wire from his mouth to the lump of plastic in his hand and only when he turned his head to the left and spat on the ground did it disappear and I felt a groaning somewhere deep inside me. He raised his shirt a little to scratch his belly and a fine trail of dark fuzz made its way beneath his navel to within his shorts; his hand followed it in for a moment as he adjusted himself. When the whistle was blown he threw the gum shield back in his mouth and turned to run in my direction with a grace that belied his bulk, his head watching at every moment as the ball made its way above the heads of twenty boys and he reached both hands up, leapt in the air, dragged it into the pit of his stomach before hoisting it back with his right hand and throwing it further down the field to some shadow whose catch I did not even turn to see.

Soon, the game ended and there was cheering on the pitch. I gathered that Mangan's team had won but it had been a close thing and a good-tempered game for the colours intermingled and there was a clasping of fists and quick hugs, hands to the back of each other's heads.

I dared to call his name as he trotted off the pitch with one of his friends and he turned to look at me, uncertain at first before a moment of recognition made him smile.

'You made it,' he said, tousling my hair as if I was a child before running on, running past me, running away, turning to his companion and laughing about something as they disappeared back towards the changing rooms and out of my sight. I stood there as the spectators started to disperse, hoping that he might come out again. He had told me to bring him an orange and I had done so but I hadn't given it to him. He hadn't even noticed it in my hand. Finally, a group of them emerged, an excitement of boys, pink-faced and wet-haired, talking and laughing loudly, sports bags slung over their shoulders, drinking cans of Coke and devouring bars of chocolate in one or two bites. Mangan among them, at their very centre.

I waited until they were all gone and walked slowly down the driveway, making my way back towards North Richmond Street, where I had no desire to be, the orange still in my hand. I was a boy uncertain where he was going, abandoned and left wandering in a part of the city that was unfamiliar to me, a place that would take me years to understand and negotiate.

That part of me that would be driven by desire and loneliness had awoken and was planning cruelties and anguish that I could not yet imagine.

Speaking in Tongues
by Emma Donoghue

"Listen," I said, my voice rasping, "I want to take you home but Dublin's a hundred miles away."

Lee looked down at her square hands. I couldn't believe she'd only spent seventeen years on this planet.

"Where're you staying?" I asked.

"Youth hostel."

I mouthed a curse at the beer-stained carpet. "I've no room booked in Galway and it's probably too late to get one. I was planning to drive back tonight. I have to be at the office by nine tomorrow."

The last of the conference goers walked past just then, and one or two nodded at me; the sweat of the *céilí* was drying on their cheeks.

When I looked back, Lee was grinning like she'd just won the lottery. "So is it comfortable in the back of your van then, Sylvia?" I stared at her. It was not the first time I had been asked that question, but I had thought that the last time would be the last.

She was exactly half my age, I reminded myself. She wasn't even an adult, legally. "As backs of vans go, yes, very comfortable."

The reason I got into that van was a poem.

I'd first heard Sylvia Dwyer on a CD of contemporary poetry in Irish. I'd borrowed it from the library to help me revise for the Leaving Cert that would get me out of convent school. Deirdre had just left me for a boy, so I was working hard.

Poem number five was called "Dhá Theanga." The woman's voice had peat and smoke in it, bacon and strong tea. I hadn't a notion what the poem was about; you needed to know how the words were spelt before you could look them up in the dictionary, and one silent consonant sounded pretty much like another to me. But I listened to the poem every night till I had to give the CD back to the library.

I asked my mother why the name sounded so familiar, and she said Sylvia must be the last of those Dwyers who'd taken over the Shanbally butchers thirty years before. I couldn't believe she was a local. I might even have sat next to her in Mass.

But it was Cork where I met her. I'd joined the Queer Soc in the first week, before I could lose my nerve, and by midterm I was running their chocolate-and-wine evenings. Sylvia Dwyer, down from Dublin for a weekend, was introduced all round by an ex of hers who taught in the French department. I was startled to learn that the poet was one of us—a "colleen," as a friend of mine used to say. Her smooth bob and silver-grey suit were intimidating as hell. I couldn't think of a word to say. I poured her plonk from a box and put the bowl of chocolate-covered peanuts by her elbow.

After that I smiled at her in Mass once when I was home in Shanbally for the weekend. Sylvia nodded back, very minimally.

Maybe she wasn't sure where she knew me from. Maybe she was praying. Maybe she was a bitch.

Of course I had heard of Lee Maloney in Shanbally. The whole town had heard of her, the year the girl appeared at Mass with a Sinead O'Connor head shave. I listened in on a euphemistic conversation about her in the post office queue but contributed nothing to it. My reputation was a clean slate in Shanbally, and none of my poems had gendered pronouns.

When I was introduced to the girl in Cork she was barely civil. But her chin had a curve you needed to fit your hand to, and her hair looked seven days old.

On one of my rare weekends at home, who should I see on the way down from Communion but Lee Maloney, full of nods and smiles. Without turning my head, I could sense my mother stiffen. In the car park afterwards she asked, "How do you come to know that Maloney girl?"

I considered denying it, claiming it was a case of mistaken identity, then I said, "I think she might have been at a reading I gave once."

"She's a worry to her mother," said mine.

It must have been after I saw Sylvia Dwyer's name on a flyer under the title DHÁ THEANGA/TWO TONGUES: A CONFERENCE ON BILINGUALISM IN IRELAND TODAY that my subconscious developed a passionate nostalgia for the language my forebears got whipped for. So I skived off my Saturday lecture to get the bus to Galway. But only when I saw her walk into that lecture theatre in her long brown leather coat, with a new streak of white across her black fringe, did I realize why I'd sat four hours on a bus to get there.

Some days I have more nerve than others. I flirted with Sylvia all that day, in the quarter hours between papers

*and forums and plenary sessions that meant equally little
to me whether they were in Irish or English. I asked her
questions and nodded before the answers had started. I told
her about Deirdre, just so she wouldn't think I was a virgin.
"She left me for a boy with no earlobes," I said carelessly.*

"Been there," said Sylvia.

*Mostly, though, I kept my mouth shut and my
head down and my eyes shiny. I suspected I was being
embarrassingly obvious, but a one-day conference didn't leave
enough time for subtlety.*

*Sylvia made me guess how old she was, and I said,
"Thirty?" though I knew from the programme note that she
was thirty-four. She said if by any miracle she had saved
enough money by the age of forty, she was going to get plastic
surgery on the bags under her eyes.*

*I played the cheeky young thing and the baby dyke
and the strong silent type who had drunk too much wine.
And till halfway through the evening I didn't think I was
getting anywhere. What would a woman like Sylvia Dwyer
want with a blank page like me?*

For a second in that Galway lecture hall I didn't
recognize Lee Maloney, because she was so out of context
among the bearded journalists and wool-skirted teachers.
Then my memory claimed her face. The girl was looking
at me like the sun had just risen, and then she stared at
her feet, which was even more of a giveaway. I stood up
straighter and shifted my briefcase to my other hand.

The conference, which I had expected to be
about broadening my education and licking up to small
Irish publishers, began to take on a momentum of its
own. It was nothing I had planned, nothing I could

stop. I watched the side of Lee's jaw right through a lecture called "Scottish Loan-Words in Donegal Fishing Communities." She was so cute I felt sick.

What was most unsettling was that I couldn't tell who was chatting up whom. It was a battle made up of feints and retreats. As we sipped our coffee, for instance, I murmured something faintly suggestive about hot liquids, then panicked and changed the subject. As we crowded back into the hall, I thought it was Lee's hand that guided my elbow for a few seconds, but she was staring forward so blankly I decided it must have been somebody else.

Over dinner—a noisy affair in the cafeteria—Lee sat across the table from me and burnt her tongue on the apple crumble. I poured her a glass of water and didn't give her a chance to talk to anyone but me. At this point we were an island of English in a sea of Irish.

The conversation happened to turn (as it does) to relationships and how neither of us could see the point in casual sex, because not only was it unlikely to be much good but it fucked up friendships or broke hearts. Sleeping with someone you hardly knew, I heard myself pronouncing in my world-weariest voice, was like singing a song without knowing the words. I told her that when she was my age she would feel the same way, and she said, Oh, she did already.

My eyes dwelt on the apple crumble disappearing, spoon by spoon, between Lee's absentminded lips. I listened to the opinions spilling out of my mouth and wondered who I was kidding. By the time it came to the poetry reading that was meant to bring the conference to a lyrical climax, I was too tired to waste time. I reached into my folder for the only way I know to say what I really mean.

Now, the word in Cork had been that Sylvia Dwyer was deep in the closet, which I'd thought was a bit pathetic but only to be expected. However.

At the end of her reading, after she'd done a few about nature and a few about politics and a few I couldn't follow, she rummaged round in her folder. "This poem gave its name to this conference," she said, "but that's not why I've chosen it." She read it through in Irish first; I let the familiar vowels caress my ears. Her voice was even better live than on the CD from the library. And then she turned slightly in her seat, and, after muttering, "Hope it translates," she read it straight at me.

> *your tongue and my tongue*
> *have much to say to each other*
> *there's a lot between them*
> *there are pleasures yours has over mine*
> *and mine over yours*
> *we get on each other's nerves sometimes*
> *and under each other's skin*
> *but the best of it is when*
> *your mouth opens to let my tongue in*
> *it's then I come to know you*
> *when I hear my tongue*
> *blossom in your kiss*
> *and your strange hard tongue*
> *speaks between my lips*

The reason I was going to go ahead and do what I'd bored all my friends with saying I'd never do again was that poem.

I was watching the girl as I read "Dhá Theanga" straight to her, aiming over the weary heads of the crowd of conference goers. I didn't look at anyone else but Lee Maloney, not at a single one of the jealous poets or Gaelgóir purists or smirking gossips, in case I might lose my nerve. After the first line, when her eyes fell for a second, Lee looked right back at me. She was leaning her cheek on her hand. It was a smooth hand, blunt at the tips. I knew the poem off by heart, but tonight I had to look down for safety every few lines.

And then she glanced away, out the darkening window, and I suddenly doubted that I was getting anywhere. What would Lee Maloney, seventeen last May, want with a scribbled jotter like me?

I sat in that smoky hall with my face half hidden behind my hand, excitement and embarrassment spiraling up my spine. I reminded myself that Sylvia Dwyer must have written that poem years ago, for some other woman in some other town. Not counting how many other women she might have read it to. It was probably an old trick of hers.

But all this couldn't explain away the fact that it was me Sylvia was reading it to tonight in Galway. In front of all these people, not caring who saw or what they might think when they followed the line of her eyes. I dug my jaw into my palm for anchorage, and my eyes locked back onto Sylvia's. I decided that every poem was made new in the reading.

If this was going to happen, I thought, as I folded the papers away in my briefcase during the brief rainfall of applause, it was happening because we were not in Dublin surrounded by my friends and work life, nor in

Cork cluttered up with Lee's, nor above all in Shanbally where she was born in the year I left for college. Neither of us knew anything at all about Galway.

If this was going to happen, I thought, many hours later as the cleaners urged Sylvia and me out of the hall, it was happening because of some moment that had pushed us over an invisible line. But which moment? It could have been when we were shivering on the floor waiting for the end-of-conference céilí band to start up, and Sylvia draped her leather coat round her shoulders and tucked me under it for a minute, the sheepskin lining soft against my cheek, the weight of her elbow on my shoulder. Or later when I was dancing like a berserker in my vest, and she drew the back of her hand down my arm and said, "Aren't you the damp thing." Or maybe the deciding moment was when the fan had stopped working and we stood at the bar waiting for drinks, my smoking hips armouring hers, and I blew behind her hot ear until the curtain of hair lifted up and I could see the dark of her neck.

Blame it on the heat. We swung so long in the *céilí* that the whole line went askew. Lee took off all her layers except one black vest that clung to her small breasts. We shared a glass of iced water and I offered Lee the last splash from my mouth, but she danced around me and laughed and wouldn't take it. Up on the balcony over the dance floor, I sat on the edge and leaned out to see the whirling scene. Lee fitted her hand around my thigh, weighing it down. "You protecting me from falling?" I asked. My voice was meant to be sardonic, but it came out more like breathless.

"That's right," she said.

Held in that position, my leg very soon began to tremble, but I willed it to stay still, hoping Lee would not feel the spasm, praying she would not move her hand away.

Blame it on the dancing. They must have got a late license for the bar, or maybe Galway people always danced half the night. The music made our bones move in tandem and our legs shake. I tried to take the last bit of water from Sylvia's mouth, but I was so giddy I couldn't aim right and kept lurching against her collarbone and laughing at my own helplessness.

"Thought you were meant to be in the closet," I shouted in her ear at one point, and Sylvia smiled with her eyes shut and said something I couldn't hear, and I said, "What?" and she said, "Not tonight."

So at the end of the evening we had no place to go and it didn't matter. We had written our phone numbers on sodden beermats and exchanged them. We agreed that we'd go for a drive. When we got into her white van on the curb littered with weak-kneed céilí dancers, something came on the radio, an old song by Clannad or one of that crowd. Sylvia started up the engine and began to sing along with the chorus, her hoarse whisper catching every second or third word. She leaned over to fasten her seat belt and crooned a phrase into my ear. I didn't understand it—something about "bóthar," or was it "máthar"?—but it made my face go hot anyway.

"Where are we heading?" I said at last, as the hedges began to narrow to either side of the white van.

Sylvia frowned into the darkness. "Cashelagen, was that the name of it? Quiet spot, I seem to remember, beside a castle."

After another ten minutes, during which we didn't meet a single other car, I realized that we were

*lost, completely tangled in the little roads leading into
Connemara. And half of me didn't care. Half of me was quite
content to bump along these lanes to the strains of late-night
easy listening, watching Sylvia Dwyer's sculpted profile out
the corner of my right eye. But the other half of me wanted
to stretch my boot across and stamp on the brake, then climb
over the gear stick to get at her.*

Lee didn't comment on how quickly I was getting us
lost. Cradle snatcher, I commented to myself, and not
even a suave one at that. As we hovered at an unmarked
fork, a man walked into the glare of the headlights.
I stared at him to make sure he was real, then rolled
down the window with a flurry of elbows. "Cashelagen?"
I asked. Lee had turned off the radio, so my voice
sounded indecently loud. "Could you tell us are we
anywhere near Cashelagen?"

The man fingered his sideburns and stepped
closer, beaming in past me at Lee. What in god's name
was this fellow doing wandering round in the middle of
the night anyway? He didn't even have our excuse. I was
just starting to roll the window up again when "Ah," he
said, "ah, if it's Cashelagen you're wanting you'd have to
go a fair few miles back through Ballyalla and then take
the coast road."

"Thanks," I told him shortly, and revved up
the engine. Lee would think I was the most hopeless
incompetent she had ever got into a van for immoral
purposes with. As soon as he had walked out of range of
the headlights, I let off the hand brake and shot forward. I glanced over at Lee's bent head. The frightening
thought occurred to me: *I could love this girl.*

The lines above Sylvia's eyebrow were beginning to swoop like gulls. If she was going to get cross, we might as well turn the radio back on and drive all night. I rehearsed the words in my head, then said them. "Sure who needs a castle in the dark?"

Her grin was quick as a fish.

"Everywhere's quiet at this time of night," I said rather squeakily. "Here's quiet. We could stop here."

"What, right here?"

Sylvia peered back at the road and suddenly wheeled round into the entrance to a field. We stopped with the bumper a foot away from a five-barred gate. When the headlights went off, the field stretched out dark in front of us, and there was a sprinkle of light that had to be Galway.

"What time did you say you had to be in Dublin?" I asked suddenly.

"Nine. Better start back round five in case I hit traffic," said Sylvia. She bent over to rummage in the glove compartment. She pulled out a strapless watch, looked at it, brought it closer to her eyes, then let out a puff of laughter.

"What time's it now?"

"You don't want to know," she told me.

I grabbed it. The hands said half past three. "It can't be."

We sat staring into the field. "Nice stars," I said, for something to say.

"Mmm," she said.

I stared at the stars, joining the dots, till my eyes watered.

And then I heard Sylvia laughing in her throat as she turned sideways and leaned over my seat belt. I heard it hissing back into its socket as she kissed me on the mouth.

When I came back from taking a pee in the bushes, the driver's seat was empty. I panicked, and stared up and down *the lane. Why would she have run off on foot? Then, with a deafening creak, the back doors of the van swung open.*

Sylvia's bare shoulders showed over the blanket that covered her body. She hugged her knees. Her eyes were bright, and the small bags underneath were the most beautiful folds of skin I'd ever seen. I climbed in and kneeled on the sheepskin coat beside her, reaching up to snap off the little light. Her face opened wide in a yawn. The frightening thought occurred to me: I could love this woman.

"You could always get some sleep, you know," I said, "I wouuln't mind." Then I thought that sounded churlish, but I didn't know how to unsay it.

"Oh, I know I could," said Sylvia, her voice melodic with amusement. "There's lots of things we could do with a whole hour and a half. We could sleep, we could share the joint in the glove compartment, we could drive to Clifden and watch the sun come up. Lots of things."

I smiled. Then I realized she couldn't see my face in the dark.

"Get your clothes off," she said.

I would have liked to leave the map-reading light on over our heads, letting me see and memorize every line of Lee's body, but it would have lit us up like a saintly apparition for any passing farmer to see. So the whole thing happened in a darkness much darker than it ever gets in a city.

There was a script, of course. No matter how spontaneous it may feel, there's always an unwritten script. Every one of these encounters has a script, even the very first time your hand undoes the button on somebody's shirt; none of us comes without expectations to this body business.

But lord, what fun it was. Lee was salt with sweat and fleshier than I'd imagined, behind all her layers of black cotton and wool. In thirty-four years I've found nothing to compare to that moment when the bare limbs slide together like a key into a lock. Or no, more like one of those electronic key cards they give you in big hotels, the open sesame ones marked with an invisible code, which the door must read and recognize before it agrees to open.

At one point Lee rolled under me and muttered, "There's somewhere I want to go," then went deep inside me. It hurt a little, just a little, and I must have flinched because she asked, " Does that hurt?" and I said, "No," because I was glad of it. "No," I said again, because I didn't want her to go.

Sylvia's voice was rough like rocks grinding on each other. As she moved on top of me she whispered in my ear, things I couldn't make out, sounds just outside the range of hearing. I never wanted to interrupt the flow by saying, "Sorry?" or "What did you say?" Much as I wanted to hear and remember every word, every detail, at a certain point I just had to switch my mind off and get on with living it. But Sylvia's voice kept going in my ear, turning me on in the strangest way by whispering phrases that only she could hear.

I've always thought the biggest lie in the books is that women instinctively know what to do to each other because their bodies are the same. None of Sylvia's shapes were the same as mine, nor could I have guessed what she was like from how she seemed in her smart clothes. And we liked different things and took things in different order, showing each other by infinitesimal movings away and movings towards. She did some things to me that I knew I wanted, some I didn't think I'd much like and didn't, and several I was startled to find that I enjoyed much more than I would have imagined. I did some things Sylvia seemed calm about, and then something she must have really needed, because she started to let out her breath in a long gasp when I'd barely begun.

Near the end, Sylvia's long fingers moved down her body to ride alongside mine, not supplanting, just guiding. "Go light," she whispered in my ear. "Lighter and lighter. Butterfly." As she began to thrash at last, laughter spilled from her mouth.

"What? What are you laughing for?" I asked, afraid I'd done something wrong. Sylvia just whooped louder. Words leaked out of her throat, distorted by pleasure.

At one point I touched my lips to the skin under her eyes, first one and then the other. "Your bags are gorgeous, you know. Promise you'll never let a surgeon at them?"

"No," she said, starting to laugh again.

"No to which?"

"No promise."

When Sylvia was touching me I didn't say a single one of the words that swam through my head. I don't know was I shy or just stubborn, wanting to make her guess what to do. The tantalization of waiting for those hands to decipher my body made the bliss build and build till when it came it threw me.

There was one moment I wouldn't swap anything for. It was in the lull beforehand, the few seconds when I stopped breathing. I looked at this stranger's face bent over me, twisted in exertion and tenderness, and I thought, Yes, you, whoever you are, if you're asking for it, I'll give it all up to you.

In the in-between times we panted and rested and stifled our laughter in the curve of each other's shoulders and debated when I'd noticed Lee and when she'd noticed me, and what we'd noticed and what we'd imagined on each occasion, the history of this particular desire. And during one of these in-between times we realized that the sun had come up, faint behind a yellow mist, and it was half five according to the strapless watch in the glove compartment.

I took hold of Lee, my arms binding her ribs and my head resting in the flat place between her breasts. The newly budded swollen look of them made my mouth water, but there was no time. I shut my mouth and my eyes and held Lee hard and there was no time left at all, so I let go and sat up. I could feel our nerves pulling apart like ivy off a wall.

The cows were beginning to moan in the field as we pulled our clothes on. My linen trousers were cold and smoky. We did none of the things parting lovers do if they have the time or the right. I didn't snatch at Lee's foot as she pulled her jeans on; she didn't sneak her head under my shirt as I pulled it over my face. The whole thing had to be over already.

It was not the easiest thing in the world to find my way back to Galway with Lee's hand tucked between my thighs. Through my trousers I could feel the cold of her fingers, and the hardness of her thumb, rubbing the linen. I caught her eye as we sped round a corner, and she grinned, suddenly very young. "You're just using me to warm your hand up," I accused.

"That's all it is," said Lee.

I was still throbbing, so loud I thought the car

was ringing with it. We were only two streets from the hostel now.

I wouldn't ask to see her again. I would just leave the matter open and drive away. Lee probably got offers all the time; she was far too young to be looking for anything heavy. I'd show her I was generous enough to accept that an hour and a half was all she had to give me. I let her out just beside the hostel, which was already opening to release some backpacking Germans. I was going to get out of the car to give her a proper body-to-body hug, but while I was struggling with my seat belt, Lee knocked on the glass. I rolled down the window, put *Desert Hearts* out of my mind, and kissed her for what I had a hunch was likely to be the last time.

I stood shivering in the street outside the hostel and knocked on Sylvia's car window. I was high as a kite and dizzy with fatigue. I wouldn't ask anything naff like when we were likely to see each other again. I would just wave as she drove away. Sylvia probably did this kind of thing all the time; she was far too famous to be wanting anything heavy. I'd show her that I was sophisticated enough not to fall for her all in one go, not to ask for anything but the hour and a half she had to give me.

When she rolled down the window, I smiled and leaned in. I shut my eyes and felt Sylvia's tongue against mine, saying something neither of us could hear. So brief, so slippery, nothing you could get a hold of.

34

DIARY OF A SCHOOL GIRL
BY MARY DORCEY

The body was in the mortuary. You would have to go
down and look beneath the coffin lid. You knew they
dressed them in the coarse brown habit of a monk.
Would you need to lean in to kiss his cold cheek? You
were told they broke the jawbone, tied it up with cloth
and sealed up all the orifices so that none of the rotting
insides could leak out. Would he have on his black
moustache still or would they have shaved him? Fergus
had told you the fingernails grew even in the grave. Your
mother said there was no need for you to come. He
would prefer you to remember him as he had been in life.

*Through all that year of 1968 I kept a diary. I kept it
secret. Even from Adrienne. At the time, it seemed a clever
invention to write in the past tense as though it all had
happened years before to someone else. Adopting this strategy
concealed me from the imagined gaze of others. And even
more from my own. One of the events that occurred in those
months I have never forgotten. But it was not, I came to see,
the most important.*

September 2nd

It was autumn, the summer over, leaves falling to the ground and the nuns waiting at the convent gate to welcome you back. School girls in purple gym-slips milled about the tree-lined avenue, throwing their berets in the air, greeting each other with thin bird-like shrieks. Adrienne was not in sight. But you knew where to find her. She'd be waiting in your secret meeting place, a deep inlet between high rocks where the nuns could swim in private without fear of being spied on.

'Well?' she said when you stood beside her.

'Well, what?' you answered to provoke her.

Sitting on the edge of the little pier where you had shared your first cigarette, her shoes and stockings taken off, she trailed her feet in the water. The blue-green sea played about her ankles, over the white arch of her instep. She wore the same gym-slip as yourself but on her it had a daring look because she left the top buttons undone, so the edge of a new white cotton bra came into view with any sudden movement of her shoulders.

'What happened to you this summer?'

'Nothing much.' Reaching her arm into the water as far as the elbow, she splashed the smooth surface, sending small rivulets travelling towards you. You spread out your hands, caught them and sent them racing back.

'But something has… I know.' Her eyes were huge and green. Dancing with mischief, your mother had said. Where had you gone, who had you seen? You had promised each other to confide anything new or strange that happened to you or anyone during the holidays. Every separation was to be put to good use, experience and sensations to be recorded and carried back as spoils to lay at each other's feet.

'I met a man.'

'A man?'

'Yes.'

'A boy, you mean?'

'No, a man.' She stared at you, her mouth wide.

'How old is he?'

'About thirty-four.'

'Thirty-four!' It was a triumph to have something to say that astonished her. She was so cool and sophisticated, so hard to shake from her poise. She was thirteen and a bit, seven months older than you. Her father was rich. He worked in England. Her mother went over every month to visit. She had no brothers or sisters so a kind of aunt who was not really an aunt came to look after her.

'Do you want to come to my place tomorrow, clever clogs? Mummy's going to London.'

Robert Maxwell was his real name but from the start Adrianne never called him anything but Mr X. He'd come back from France at Easter but you only got to know him in the summer. You met him in the library one Monday morning in July. You called in several days a week because you read books so quickly and the long holidays were boring. He took a copy of *Wuthering Heights* from the top bookcase. 'Take this—it might teach you something useful.' You had read it already but you didn't say so. Miss Cadogan, the librarian, smiled. There was no need to have it stamped, she whispered. After that you saw him in the newsagent's and once in the Post Office. He went to the library most days and picked out books at random because he was a dilettante, he said, the master of his own time and caprice.

You ran through the school gates at half three, a hundred of you or more, in your short skirted uniforms, wild with the exhilaration of sudden liberty: the fresh wind, the air on your bare legs, the cry of the gulls, the smell of the apple trees that bordered the drive. You were worse than pagans, Mother Benignus said at Assembly, racing and cackling, like a flock of geese set loose from a farmyard. Mrs. Coughlan had seen you from the door of the newsagents.

September 4th

'It's terrible, once you've got a man into your blood!' Adrienne read in a posh English voice. 'A man in your blood.' It made you laugh out loud.

It was Friday, the third day of the new term. You sat on your bicycles, leaning against the stone wall of the convent. Adrienne had propped her feet on the handlebars. The muscles of her calf were smooth and brown-skinned. She was reading aloud pages from *Lady Chatterley's Lover*. She'd stolen it from her parents' wardrobe where they stored everything they wanted to hide. 'What's his name, this auld fellow you've met?'

'Robert."

'What does he look like?'

'He has blue eyes and black hair.'

'Not white hair?'

'I said he's thirty-four not seventy.' In fact, you didn't know exactly what age he was. He never talked about himself. Only about books or paintings, ideas and stories, characters he had known in London and Paris. That was why you liked him. Everything about him was different from ordinary, boring people.

'Still. That's ancient. How can you possibly like someone who's ancient?'

'He's a friend, not a boyfriend so it doesn't matter.'

Commanding you to return her look, she stared at you. This was the extraordinary thing that started the first day you met. You didn't know which of you began it but you could hold each other's gaze in a long, unwavering stare until it felt like you would sink into the other's brain and read their thoughts.

'When is your father coming home?'

'Don't know.'

'Why?'

She dropped her nearly finished cigarette on the ground and stamped it out with her heel.

'Have to dash. Mummy's waiting.' She revved the pedals of her bike and raced towards the town without looking back or waving.

You were never sure what she'd do next. She was more changeable than anyone, on some days cool and aloof, on others giddy and affectionate. Scatter-brained, Mother Carmel said. Too pretty for her own good, Mother Loyola said.

September 12th

On the next fine day he would take you to Powerscourt to see the Waterfall, Mr X promised. If he had your mother's permission. He gave you a fountain pen, a copy of the Works of Oscar Wilde and a box of oil paints in a black enamel box. He was an artist. He had studied in Berlin. He made landscapes in dark colours with strange figures that were not animal or human. They looked out from behind trees or with their faces staring up from under the sea. He told you he would paint you one day when you were older. No one who saw you talking together asked anything about it or why you had become friends because you were only a child and everyone in the town knew him to see. He was a gentleman, well-educated and of private means, Mrs. Fogarty from the post office told your mother.

The nuns forbade many things for no reason you could see but to just as many prohibitions they turned a blind eye. You were told not to congregate about the convent gates after school or to do your homework in a friend's house. They warned against the dangers of particular friendships but allowed you to sit beside a best friend in the concert hall when the lights went out, to watch a film projected on a trembling sheet they used for a screen. They paid no notice when you danced close with a special friend in the ballroom on winter evenings after study when each girl had her sets already organised from the day before like a heroine in Pride and Prejudice.

September 19th

'Does it make you sad—even though it's three years?'
　　You were sitting on the top deck of the 7A bus, going to Adrienne's house for tea, passing the hospital

where your father had died. You both made the sign of the cross. You knew there was a chapel behind the carpark.

You looked up at the window on the second floor where your father's bed used to be.

'Sometimes.'

'Did you see him afterwards?'

'No. Mam went with Fergus.'

You were glad she asked. Most people didn't say anything when you told them what had happened except, 'Sure you're a child and a child couldn't understand'. Sometimes if they didn't know he was dead and asked what he did for a living, to save yourself trouble you would say: 'He's a harpist.'

'The house is weird now. My mother often cries when no one is looking.'

Adrienne lit a cigarette she had pinched from her mother's handbag. 'You can come to my place any day, clever clogs.' She took the first draw from the Rothmans, then blew smoke into your eyes. 'I've something I need to tell you. If you promise not to repeat it to a single living soul.'

'I never tell people.' No one would ask because they knew you were best friends. Your names began with the same letter so your desks were side by side, you shared your sandwiches at break, walked home together and copied each other's homework at the weekend.

'Cross your heart and hope to die!'

You moved your right thumb slowly over your chest.

'I don't know if I want to say it now.' Her look was accusing as if you had already broken your word. 'Maybe I won't tell you ever.'

'Why not? We always share things...' But you didn't finish the sentence. You thought of Mr X, all the subjects you talked about with him that you hadn't confided.

September 22nd

The next weekend he took you to a matinee performance of *The Field* by John B. Keane. When you came out into the sharp light of day at five o' clock he was angry. 'It was all too typical of this festering country, fighting for centuries over an acre of land that wouldn't feed a goat. Small minded and vicious. A nation of peasants who drove out every free thinker and artist. Not that my lot are much better, hunting and shooting Prods mainly', he said, 'philistines and proud of it but one or two had imagination. And fortunately we had a library in the house. That is the only way to liberate your mind. Reading.' He asked if you had started on the Oscar Wilde yet. 'Now there was a brave man, ridiculed in this papal state. There is no such thing as an immoral book, he had said, only one well written or a badly written.'

At one moment you were a child, at the next an adult. You could move from one state to another in an instant, on a whim and back again without anyone noticing. It was that fleeting interval when grown-ups neither talked or listen to you. You were too young to comprehend, they said. No one apart from the nuns expected consistency in your actions or emotions.

You were blasphemous and immodest, governed neither by

*the laws of God or man, Mother Loyola declared, standing
in front of the class on Monday morning, a disgrace to your
religion. One girl had been seen laughing outside the chapel
door, splashing others with holy water from the baptismal
font. It was hysteria, pure hysteria, theatrics and drama.
Empty vessels make the most noise. She could guess the culprits.*

September 28th

In three days' time you would be thirteen. Almost
grown-up, Adrienne said, and you talked of adventures
you dreamed of having, all kinds of things, anything daft
or dangerous; stowing away on planes or cargo ships,
disguising yourselves as boys or gypsies to walk about at
night in forbidden streets, talking to foreigners.

'Why is Mr X always mooning around? Does he think
you're not safe on your own?' Adrienne had seen him
the afternoon before, passing the school gate. She
always noticed everything without needing to pay
attention. He looked mysterious with his greying hair,
she said, like someone from the movies. 'And why does
he smoke cigars?'

'Because he's a bohemian.' Colm had taught
you the word and explained about men and women
who ignored convention and lived abroad, dedicated to
art and to truth. 'Is he English? He wears a ring on his
finger. An Irish man would never do that.'

He was English. But for some reason you didn't
want to say so. 'Well, he's a black Prod anyway, that's
nearly as good.' Adrienne talked about most things as if

they were a great joke or very boing because she knew
so much about the world. But about some subjects you
understood more because you read books, history and
novels and she didn't.

'He looks romantic,' Sally Byrne said, 'with his
trench coat and his broody eyes, like the spy who came in
from the cold.'

'He's better looking than any of our fathers,'
Jacinta Barry said.

'Dilapidated,' Adrienne said.

October 5th

On Saturday afternoon, four days after your birthday,
Mr X raised his wine glass at the table and told you that
your eyes were beautiful. You were sitting opposite him
having dinner in the Royal hotel beside his golf club at
Kilmurray. You were eating fried egg, sausage and chips
when he made this extraordinary pronouncement. Your
heart swelled with pride. For an adult to find anything
praiseworthy about your appearance was an entirely
foreign notion. He had driven the slow way in his dark
green Morris Minor twelve miles from your house, along
winding country roads. Before leaving, he phoned your
mother to ask her permission. It was very kind of him,
she said. It was good for you to have adult company these
days because you missed your father.

It was a long room with a high ceiling. There
was a candle on every table and a blue vase in front of a
mirror filled with flowers. You sat still, unblushing, as his
gaze rested on your face. You didn't want to disturb this

strange new tension but the next words he spoke startled you even more, 'How many other men will look across a table and tell you this?' His own eyes were sad and his voice solemn. A thrill of recognition passed through you. An astonishing vista entered your mind, like a scene from a romantic film: hallways softly lit, lowered voices, something half-glimpsed when you opened the door of a room without warning and adults fell silent. The weird idea came to you, there might be no need to do anything in particular to win affection or make things happen in the grown-up world. It might be enough to sit still on one side of a table and allow somebody's gaze to rest on yours and this magical atmosphere could be created by a word or glance from some undercurrent that must be hidden just below the ordinary surface.

You asked him to tell you what he liked about your eyes. You needed all the information. Without exact details, corroborating evidence of some kind, Adrienne would never believe you. But he turned away, 'There's no need to fish. It's enough that they are and that you don't know why. That's your charm. Don't be in a hurry to lose it.'

October 6th

'I hope Mr. Maxwell is still going to church?' your mother asked.

'But he's a protestant?'

'Yes, but they are good people too. He asked my permission before he took you to his golf club, you know. I hope you behaved yourself? Your father wouldn't have

45

allowed you so much freedom, but I'm afraid it might only make you more defiant if I try to limit it.'

You were giving her a hand to change the beds. She was putting clean sheets on all of them. The day before, you had helped her to carry them in from the line, to iron and fold each one before putting them in the hot-press to air.

'Perhaps I confided in you too much, after your father's death. When I was heartbroken myself. I spoke my thoughts aloud because you were a child still and wouldn't fully understand. It was harder for your older brothers. I didn't want to put extra weight on their shoulders.' She took down two frocks from the wardrobe. She held them up to her face at the dressing table mirror, a red and a blue.

'What do you think? I haven't entirely lost my looks, have I?'

'You look nice.'

'What would you think if I were to marry again?'

'Did somebody ask you?'

'Not in so many words. But people do say I shouldn't leave it too late.'

'If you were married to a man, would he be my father?'

'Not in the same way that Daddy was.'

'Would he move in with us?'

'I suppose he could, unless he had a bigger house himself.'

'Would he give us orders? Would he tell Colm what time to come home? Would he correct my homework?'

'He might, depending on what kind of man he was.'

'Well, I don't want another father.'

'It will soon be three years. I can't be on my own forever, you know.'

.

October 14th

You were walking home from the ten o'clock Mass, when Mr X came out of Madigan's pub.

'I think my time was better spent than yours.' He was going down to the little pier near the convent to fish. He asked if you'd like to come.

'I have to eat dinner early on a Sunday.'

He was planning to go to France in a few months' time, he said. Had you ever been to the continent? He would like to bring you but it wouldn't be proper.

'Why not?'

'People wouldn't think it right. They would talk.'

You didn't understand. It didn't matter to you what people thought. You were always in trouble anyway even when you did nothing. It would be good to have a reason for once. He laughed when you said this and shook his head.

'My mother asked if you still went to church.'

'Your mother is an admirable woman. She's fortunate to have the consolation of faith.'

'Do you not believe in God?' You felt a thrill of danger saying this.

'It depends on what you mean by God. I was like most people once. I believed in him when he was on my side. Not when he wasn't.'

'What about now?'

'Now, I have the virtue of consistency at least.'

'What happened?'

'You're too young to understand.'

'Why do adults only say that when they want to keep secrets?'

'Would you like to come for a spin on the motorbike on Sunday? I'm going to make some drawings at the Ecclesiastical site.'

October 19th

At Glendalough you walked all around the upper lake and came back to see the ruins of the ancient monastic village. It was the university of its day, the monks were farmers, scholars and contemplatives. They built the Round Tower as a refuge to escape from Viking raiders. He took pictures of the cathedral and the deer who mingled with ragged sheep in the lake field and a heron standing on one leg under the stone bridge. He would make copies to give your mother. He brought you to the great Celtic cross. If you could reach your arms round it, you could make a special wish. The column of stone was too wide for you to have a chance but he helped you by stretching his own hands round to meet yours. Then he lifted you up to sit on the highest tombstone. He'd take a photograph first and make a sketch from it at home. He settled the collar of your blouse to frame your face. He took one picture from a distance and another close up. He raised the hem of your skirt, carefully between his forefinger and thumb, so that it rested just clear of your knees. When he brushed your fringe back from your eyes his mouth came

close to your cheek. You heard his breathing. You waited
to see what he wanted. He put his arms around you as
if he was about to lift you down. His tweed jacket was
rough against your cheek. His hands rested flat just below
your shoulder blades. You thought he was going to kiss
you but he didn't. He leaned back suddenly and looked
away. "Forgive me," he said. You did not want to forgive
him. You wanted him to kiss you now that you thought
he might. To show you how. You thought he might be
the best person you could find to teach you.

October 21st

'I think Mr X is making you boring.' Adrianne's was
standing at the window showing off the new nylon slip
her mother had bought in London. It was white and see-
through. You saw the outline of her breasts. They had
grown quite suddenly in the night. She just woke up one
morning and there they were. 'Aren't they terrific?' she
grinned with pride. They were perfectly round and pale
and the nipples were pink. She'd envied you because you
had begun to get yours already but now you were even.
You wanted to tell her about Glendalough. You tried to
remember Mr X's expression, to imitate how he'd looked
at you but you couldn't find the right words. She was
staring at herself in the mirror pretending she'd forgotten
you.

     'I think my mother is having a secret love affair.'
     'Who with?'
     'Uncle Jack.
     'Your uncle Jack!'

'I came into the sitting room three nights ago. They were standing, doing nothing in the dark. He had his arms round her. She was crying.'

'She was probably just sad.'

'It wasn't that kind of crying. She had that look women are supposed to get'.

'What look?'

'Moony. I think she might be *preggers.*'

'But your father's been away for months!'

'*X-act-ally!*'

You were still trying to decide how to tell her about Glendalough but you felt peculiar. You didn't want to get it mixed up with her mother and uncle. You hadn't seen Mr X for ages. He hadn't come to the back gate at the school or to the library. You hadn't really noticed much because you were distracted by Adrienne's new interest in boys.

'Do you want to go to Peter Conroy's party on Saturday?' You had been saving this up to impress her.

'Where?'

'His parents. Their gigantic house. They're away and there's a private lane that leads to the beach.'

'*Supperr-beh.*' This was her new word for everything she admired. She said it in the French way imitating Mother Etienne pouting her lips when she taught the importance of stress in Latin languages.

'How do you know him?'

'Fergus and Colm.'

'You're so lucky to have brothers. You've everything that's useful. I'm stuck here being my mother's only child. It's quite *dee-manding.*'

October 29th

Black stubble had grown on his cheeks. The rest of his face was a red blotchy colour. It was ten days since you'd seen him. He was coming out of the library and you were bringing back books for your mother, novels by Elizabeth Bowen and Agatha Christie. You'd read them both in bed at night with a torch.

'Hello stranger.'

'Have you been away somewhere?'

'I've been busy. A bit seedy, if truth be told.'

'How do you mean?'

'In my case, it means visiting remote country hotels to have one over the eight.'

'Why are you doing that?'

'Stop your questions child. I've got something to give you. Just for you—do not show it to another living being. Swear it?' He handed you a blue envelope. You thought you felt the edge of a card inside.

'Have you got your motorbike? Could we go to the Coolmine?'

'Not today. I've work to do.'

'Tomorrow then?'

'Possibly.' He touched his hand to his hat like an actor on a stage, turned away and walked towards the town.

You didn't read the letter until you were on your own. You went down to the pier and sat on a bollard. You watched the waves rolling past the harbour. Were they the same waves you saw here the day before and the day before that? Did they go round and round in endless circles from one side of the bay to the other? Or could the same waves end up in Wales or even France? You liked to think about this. It was the kind of mystery you found consoling. You had thought of it often after your father died. You could disappear for hours. When you went in, your mother would ask where you'd been. 'Watching the sea and thinking.' She accepted this as a good explanation and didn't ask more questions.

You tore the envelope open with the edge of your nail. You drew out one sheet of stiff white paper.
'I apologise for my conduct when we visited the graveyard. It was a moment of self-indulgence for which I'm sincerely sorry. I hope I didn't frighten you in any way. But you are an intelligent girl and will come to understand. It's only that you remind me of my own little daughter, Paloma, my only child who died when she was almost the age you are now. I prayed to god to spare her. I went down on my knees but he let her die anyway, the charlatan.

I won't see you for some time. I've to go to London on business. Be good. Remember to keep reading and preserve your enquiring mind.
Robert.'

November 8th

In the sitting room by the bay window your mother was reading *Great Expectations* when you came in. She read it again every year. The characterisation of Miss Havisham was what made it a classic. She had heard in the Post Office that Colette O'Connor who had left school at fifteen without explanation, was in fact pregnant, as some gossips had suspected from the first. The poor girl, she said. You didn't pay much attention because you had met some new, quite interesting boys when you went to the Saturday disco at St Michaels. You danced with them both and made a date for coffee at the Buzz-Club. 'It's great to be grown-up at last, isn't it? To be able to do what we like?' Adrienne said.

You dated them again by the bandstand in the park. You let them sit with their arms around you. Adrienne's opinion was you should let their hands explore your body as far as your waist. Brian wanted to kiss but you didn't want to. Instead you allowed his hands to move up and down your back and he put one hand on your breast for three seconds. Later going home, Adrienne complained that James was too stupid and didn't know what to do.

'Why do all boys have spots and angry-looking red necks and why are they *so borrring*? You could almost miss Mr X. At least he didn't go pink in the face when he looked at you.'

'Older is definitely better.'

'That's why I've made a date with Andrew. He's sixteen.'

'You never told me!"

'I met him in the Roma. He's very good looking!' You turned away pretending to search for something on the bookshelf.

'Yesterday he kissed me.'

'Why?'

'It was a great kiss too. He used his tongue.'

November 12th

You were rowing across the Sound to the island.
Adrienne was sitting in the stern trailing her hand in the
sea. It was the last day you could go before all the boats
were taken up for winter.

'Do you believe in God? Do you believe he's wise
and just? That he'd always help anyone who prayed to him?'

'Isn't that what he's for? What would be the point
of a God who isn't wise?'

'But why does he let such horrible things happen?
Even to people who pray all day, nuns and priests?'

'I can't imagine anything happening to nuns.
Good or bad. Nothing does. All they ever pray for is fine
weather for the match, easy papers in the Inter Cert and
a peaceful release.' She tossed her hair back from her
shoulder with a haughty face, like a pony.

You told her about the letter. The part about his
daughter.

'What is he apologising for? What's wrong with
his daughter being dead—it wasn't his fault?' She was
annoyed, you could see. You tried to think of a way to
explain about the afternoon in the churchyard. But your
throat was dry and your skin felt cold.

'How long is it since you saw him?' She was
reading your mind as usual. 'It seems like ages.'

'The day we went to Glendalough. He was very
different.'

'Did he try something or what?'

'No.'

'Did you want him to?'

'It felt funny. The way he stared at me.'

'You must be in *luvve!*'

'Don't be completely stupid!'

'He's probably just a dirty old man. My mother is always warning me. You're lucky that he's good looking. All I ever get is the old fellow who sticks his thing through his trousers when I'm walking across the Park. Mummy says he should be locked up. But he's only pathetic, his big stupid face and his long red thing hanging out like a dog panting.'

You changed the subject to the party on Saturday after the new film at the Adelphi. Adrienne said she'd teach you the French Lurch. She'd learned it on her holiday in Bordeaux. 'I want to impress Andrew with my latest acquisitions.' She cupped her breasts in her hands as if they were ripe apples or oranges she was offering.

You pulled into the wooden jetty on the island and shipped the oars. You jumped to shore and moored the boat with a reef knot.

'Oh, look at you! Bravo, clever clogs.'

*

The weeks passed slowly then, the light grew dim, the days shorter. The end of term examination was talked of. Adrienne was told to come straight home from school every afternoon to study. You went to the library to read where it was quiet. You studied books that Fergus recommended, novels by French and Russian writers, stories of revolution, heroism and betrayal. You liked to sit in the half-light, looking onto the street where strangers passed. You bided your time, dreaming and indolent. You imagined the future to come, exotic countries, exciting people, intellectuals who talked only of history, novels and love.

*

December 1st

It was already dark and the light was on in the kitchen. Your mother was stirring soup at the stove. She had her thoughtful, far-away face.

'I heard sad news today.'

You took off your school bag and gave her your full attention.

'What?'

'Just that someone we used to know has died.'

'Who?'

'Robert Maxwell.'

'Mr X?'

'Yes.'

'Died?'

'I'm afraid so. Mrs Morgan in the Newsagents told me. It seems he'd come back after a long stay in England. Two weeks ago. But he hardly left the house. He was drinking. One afternoon he bought a bottle of whiskey at Madigan's. He said he was going to the Black Rock to fish. They think he must have fallen into the water after dark. There was no chance anyone could have saved him. His body was found yesterday. We must pray for him. He had no family that we can discover. There's no one to go to the mortuary to identify the body. I offered to go. I did know him a little.'

'Would you like me to come, Mam? I haven't seen him for ages.'

'No love, it can't make any difference to poor Robert now. He'd prefer you to remember him as he was. Such a handsome man and very kind to you. He had a good life, I think, the one he wanted, the life of an artist, which isn't always easy.'

You had a dream that night when you were asleep in bed. You were fishing from the pier with Colm and your line got caught in seaweed. When you pulled it up you saw a man's head coming out of the water, caught on the hook. His mouth opened wide and he called your name but you were stuck to the ground and could not move your feet or speak.

December 14th

The afternoons then were really the evenings because it was the second week of December. You got off the bus near the Adelphi and went to the Buzz-Club. Adrienne was sitting at a corner table, drinking black coffee from a little white cup because she had lived in France until she was eight.

'Will we go for a stroll on the pier instead of the film?' You turned down onto the coast road. In front of you the sun was shining on the rocks and behind the steeples of the two churches glittered as it they had turned into gold.

Two of the trawler men you knew by sight were sitting on lobster pots, drinking tea from enamel mugs and smoking their pipes.

'Good evening girls.'

'We want a bad evening, not a good one.'

'What would your fathers say if they heard you?'

'We don't have fathers. They're dead long ago.'

'Aren't you the rascals, the pair of you? How do your poor mothers manage?'

'We don't have mothers either.' Adrienne pinched your arm. You loved these flights of fancy, her giddy leaps into nonsense, the way she made jokes at awful things to wake people up.

You had almost reached the middle point of the pier. The wind was cold. You stopped to lean against the wall. Adrienne moved closer and her elbow pressed against yours. The beam from the lighthouse was circling the bay like a golden scarf thrown across the sea, splashing over the rocks as it went from east to west.

'My mother says we'll have to do things differently when my father comes home.'

'Why?'

'I was right about her. She isn't pregnant but she *was* having something with Uncle Jack.'

'How do you know?'

'My father wrote to me. They've decided to send me to boarding school.'

'Where?'

'Somewhere down the country. Waterford maybe?'

You were struck dumb. You turned your face away.

'Would you mind?' She looked straight into your eyes. 'Awfully?'

Your chest was tight. 'Yes.'

Your breath caught in your throat.

'Would you have to make friends with Dolores Keogh and Philomena Tubridy? And help Carmel Flanagan with her homework and smell her horrible dusty, long, straggly, mousey hair when she combs it?' This was the funniest thing you could imagine. It sent you both into rings of giggles.

'Remember Carmel asking me once what I put on my skin to make it glossy? Why would anyone say that?'

A trawler was coming through the harbour mouth with a putt-putting noise from the engine. Seagulls streamed from the mast like a banner.

'Because it's beautiful,' you answered, brave for the first time that day. It was such an unusual thing to say you had to keep very still.

'Yours is nice too. But you're luckier.'

'Why?'

'Andrew said he thought you were sexy.'

Your heart began to beat too fast. It hurt. You turned to look behind her at a big orange cat creeping along the south wall.

'She must have seen something,' you said to distract yourself, 'the way she's skulking, a rat maybe.'

'Funny, if you changed one letter in their name they'd be the same. Men and women are like that, just two letters in the difference. Do you think they really *are* different inside?'

You knew she wanted a proper answer. 'I think maybe, inside everyone there are two people. Inside a woman and inside a man there's two people.'

Adrianne crumpled up her nose, 'You're weird

sometimes clever clogs, you know. So *profound.*'

Her hand was resting on the wall beside yours. Even her fingers were tanned.

'It's sad that Mr X died. Did you go to the funeral?'

'Mam said it was better to think of him as he was.'

'What happened exactly?'

'He fell off the rocks. He was fishing. My mother had to identify him.'

'Where was his family?'

'He didn't have any. But a cousin came from Scotland.'

'My father told me drowning was the quickest death and he was in the navy. The cold water makes you slip away until you're unconscious.'

A woman on the slip below was walking with a white terrier. 'If I got a new dog, if it was small, Mam says I could keep her in my bedroom at night. I'd love one.'

Adrienne had an expression you hadn't seen before. 'I'm sorry about Mr X.' She nudged your shoulder with hers. 'Does it feel horrible?'

'Not that much. I didn't see him for a long time.' You took a deep breath and uttered something that was on your mind since your mother told you. 'Do you think he might have been angry with me? Because of forgetting about him?'

'Don't be idiotic. Why would he care? Wasn't it only a month you didn't see him?'

'Longer.'

'I wonder what he looks like now? Is his skin yellow and stiff like the mummies we saw in St Michens?' This was to make you laugh but you wished she hadn't said it. You knew bodies were kept in the mortuary so the smell wouldn't start until they were buried. Fergus had explained all this when your father died. The image from your dream came back again, the face grinning from under the sea. You needed to do something wild, dangerous to block out the pictures in your head.

Suddenly, a shower of rain began, pelting down on your heads, beating as hard as stones on the granite ground. 'Race you to the end.' Adrienne slapped you on the back to get you started. You ran like mad things, shrieking, spinning your arms as if you were windmills. Your shoes clattered on the stone and your breath came blowing out in clouds.

'Beat you.' She almost collapsed against you when you reached the lighthouse. Both of you were panting. You sat down on a high wooden bench, pressed against the wall for shelter and swung your legs over the side. You couldn't find the words to say what you were thinking.

'Did Mr X truly never kiss you?'

'No.'

'That's a pity.'

'Why?'

'It would have been practice.'

You clenched your hands between your knees until they were numb.

'Wouldn't it be funny if we did?' Adrienne asked.

'Did what?'

'If we practiced?'

'What?

'Kissing.'

The beam of the lighthouse shone an enormous arc of golden light across the waves. You felt shivery and hot in the same moment.

'Oh that.' You stopped breathing and gripped your arms about your chest.

'It would be an adventure wouldn't it?'

The waves crashed against the pier where the mouth of the harbour opened. You felt the spray on your bare knees. It was cold and it calmed your blood. Two fishermen were standing at the bow of the trawler. The tall one was washing down the deck with a red yard brush, the other was stacking wooden crates.

'They didn't catch much,' you said. Adrienne leaned slowly, close to your shoulder. When her face was almost touching yours she went still. She smiled straight into your eyes. You nearly jumped back in fright. She pouted her lips then and put them against yours. They were warm and soft and tasted of the coffee she had bought at the Roma. You pressed your own lips tight to hers and let them soften again. Her hands on your waist pulled you close. Her heart was throbbing. You tried to think of all you would learn. And then your mind went numb and you forgot to think. Her breath merged with yours. It was warm and sweet. Her tongue was at the edge of your mouth.

All at once you felt sure and powerful. You took her face between your hands the way you had seen in the movies. Blown by the wind a flock of kittiwakes went screeching over your head. It was a slow, deep kiss. It had to be perfect because it was the first. And because you wanted her to like it as much as you did.

BRAIDED RIVER
BY NEIL HEGARTY

'And I'll help you,' Gerry says. 'Go to sleep now.'

In the past, as you know, I wouldn't have been a great one for talk of turning points and pivots. This sort of thinking left me – *cold*, I was going to say, though *annoyed* is closer to the mark. Or *impatient*, or *vexed*. I could go on.

Instead, I wanted the evidence. I was a proof addict. I know better, now.

We met in the middle of the night, Gerry and I, and that was one turning point, one pivot.

We pretended we were night owls by nature, congratulating ourselves that first evening on this synchronicity. It would be fifteen years ago now – 'fifteen years, Brian, imagine!' Pauline said – when we ended up in an all-night coffee place off St Martin's Lane. We'd been clubbing, me with my friends and Gerry with his; ears still ringing, and voices still ragged.

'This one? This looks OK,' Gerry said, and I nodded, and in we went. We were easy and familiar already in that way that the straights don't entirely understand.

'What did you chat about?' Pauline wanted to know.

'Everything. Lots of things. We just chatted.' I felt the familiar irritation that Pauline generated within me – and besides which, where to begin? We'd talked about everything. I told him about my rivers, about Dublin. Even about Donal.

And he reciprocated.

I felt I was breathing properly, for the first time in months – no, in years.

We talked until five o'clock in the morning, then we swapped numbers; meet the very next day. A goodbye, very casual, outside St Martin in the Fields. A pinker-than-pink dawn breaking over Trafalgar Square, and I took this to be a good sign.

And who made the suggestion to meet again? – was another of Pauline's: but neither of us had, the next day was already a given, there was a flow, something momentous had already taken place. So I shut her down, you might say. 'I see,' she said.

Going our separate ways that first night, me heading north and Gerry south of the river. Turning after ten or fifteen seconds for another look and a smile, then turning again for home and bed.

The decorousness of it.

Decorous was Pauline's word.

'Your separate ways! So decorous! Such gents!' she said down the phone. I could see that she was – as usual, I thought – trying to stake her claim in the proceedings. She liked to set the tone, even from afar: and the tone in this case was *decorous*. She'd phoned, too early, for 'the *goss*, the *craic*, oh tell me *everything*,' and there I was – again, as usual – giving her too little detail. 'Scanty,' she said. 'You'll have to do better than that.'

Her point – and it had been often repeated over the years, because she was pleased with having come up with the metaphor – was that as a geographer I should be a whole lot better at describing detailed terrains, by which she meant detailed conversations.

'Well, we're meeting again this evening,' I said, and she seemed mollified. 'So, let's hope I'll have more to tell you tomorrow,' I said – and I did. A bit more. A little bit.

So, ostensibly night owls when we met, Gerry and I – but definitely not night owls all these years later. Now, our true habits and patterns are familiar and smooth with use. Such as this night. I like to – Pauline would be pleased to know this – go over the terrain after an evening out, to conduct a survey as to who was there and who said what to whom, and when.

And so, this survey – which seems at first no different.

We're such romantics. Now, Gerry takes off his shoes and socks with a groan – new shoes – and then drops his trousers and pants too. He stands in the bath clad only in his shirt, turns on the taps – Goldilocks, how are you: not too hot and not too cold, just right. The water gushes over his feet, he wiggles his toes, and I sit on the edge of the bath, and watch the water flow and vanish.

'Oh, better, thank God for that,' he says, and I hand him the towel and he dries his feet: then, we move from bathroom to bedroom, and Gerry sits on his side of the bed and massages spearmint cream into his feet, slips on his thin bed socks. 'What a sexpot I am,' he says, and then adds that you wouldn't want the cream staining the duvet cover, which is what he always says, and I say what I always say in reply.

'Stains aren't always bad.'

'Very true.'

We're going through it all. Pauline's new house, New Year party, fellow guests, the usuals. The buffet: the ham baked and sliced 'wafer-thin', the potatoes sprinkled with something nice – 'it was za'atar,' Gerry says, 'we should get some of that' – and the nut loaf for the vegetarians, the blueberry meringue. 'Don't call it an Eton mess,' Pauline said to the multitude. 'We don't like the word Eton, sure we don't,' and we talk about that too, about Pauline's flabby liberalism, which never convinces. A little snow, even, falling faintly like chaff on the way home. In the morning, a further postmortem awaits, a more detailed survey. All as usual.

'Pauline was flying,' Gerry says, and I say that yes, Pauline was wired to the moon.

Outside, London's skies crackle still with fireworks, and now I turn out the light, and we spoon in the darkness. 'Happy New Year,' and 'Happy New Year.'

Tonight is like every other night.

*

The party has already shifted into third gear when we arrive. The house is on a side street off another side street off the Holloway Road, and is new to us: Pauline, with her Alex, got the keys just a couple of days before Christmas, and she has seen to it that nobody has set foot inside the place. Until tonight. It must be perfect: her New Year party must be a Supreme Unveiling, which is a highly Pauline thing to say.

Gerry rolled his eyes about this. Pauline has never been completely his friend; she was originally my friend, my flatmate, I had followed her from Dublin to London, or so her version of the story went; and this distinction has remained intact as the years have passed. He thinks her too dramatic: but his essential kindness always comes through, and so he added, 'But no, why not, good for her.'

I don't know about that. Too much drama is not my thing.

'Go easy on her,' Gerry sometimes says, and frowns.

So, a new house, although the party is far from new. Pauline has hosted a New Year party for as long as anyone can remember, ever since our crowd shifted, in blocks and groups and ones and twos and couples, from post-university Dublin over to London, to set ourselves up in professions and partnerships and on the property ladder. Pauline has hosted us – this year in this bigger unveiled house, which really has been made possible by Alex and his money – annually, and we have always attended, the whole crowd attends. We're all held together by some affection – sometimes though not always – but also by habit, by references to the past, by the patterns and passage of exile.

Gerry spotted this.

'*Do you remember* and *do you remember*,' he from time to time sing-songs. But I like this remembering and remembering, this examining of layers of time, this looking afresh, it appeals to the professional side of me. All the sediment held, suspended – though of course, it depends on what you want to remember.

'And you're an academic, Pauline tells me,' Alex observed, the first time he was presented for viewing.

'That's right,' I dutifully said. 'I lecture in geography.'

'She tells me you're been jetting off all round the globe. Alaska, she tells me —'

'Adding to my carbon footprint: yes, I'm afraid that's right,' because I feel a bit testy about that side of things — or rather, testy about people mentioning it. 'But sadly there's no help for it. I study what they call braided rivers, and there's only so many of them in the world, and none of them are in north London.' Which seemed to shut him up: still, he'd been civil, he'd made an effort; make an effort too, I thought.

Off the Holloway Road, then, and right and left and left again: and there's the house, lit from top to toe. A narrow London house and not large, or not too large: mid-Victorian, yellow brick, two-storey over basement, with steep steps up to the front door. We've already checked it out, needless to say, on Google Earth: rotating the view, all the angles, noting the back garden, or rather, yard. Of course this side of the Holloway Road doesn't go in for large houses — that's the west side, the Holloway Road is a divide in the city, says I the geographer, it's not unlike a flowing river, a bit muddy, and now with the added feature of Pauline deposited on its eastern shore. I detect within myself relief that Pauline is enthroned in a house that is largely the same in scale and form as our own house. Had she been established in a larger house — well, that might have been a bit more difficult to bear.

Lit up like a lighthouse, this evening. There's the Christmas tree shining silver in the ground-floor bow window, and the front door wide open, hospitable, light flowing out and down the steps, and there's Pauline in its frame, and shadows moving behind her in the narrow hall.

Pauline's hair is still long, still – with a little help – dark, as dark as when I first met her: it's her signal feature, as I very well know, and tonight it bounces and curls as she descends a step, as we ascend, as she kisses and kisses. 'My lovely boys, you came!' she carols – as if there has ever been any question of us not coming – and shoves us delicately up the final step and into the hall.

Always, always a great affair, Pauline's annual party. Never once has it fallen flat. Everyone comes, she sees to that side of things; she whips and whips, and there is always – I do see this – a generosity to the whole endeavour. Take tonight, where this generosity communicates itself in the feast of candlelight, the Christmas tree sparkling, a promise of mountains of excellent food and waterfalls, Niagaras of booze.

She is a good egg, Pauline.

So I tell anyone who asks.

A good egg, a good egg. And she can laugh at herself. One year, one notorious time, she took seriously, just for a moment, a Martha Stewart recipe calling for a ham to be baked on a bed of grass. This would be her big thing for the party. But, 'It says I have to find an organic meadow and cut the grass myself,' she said and frowned, so englamoured by that ghastly fantasia of a cookbook that she lost her reason. Where would she find an organic meadow in London at the end of December? Momentarily lost her reason, and we watched as the glamour faded in the course of three or four seconds. ('Christ,' I could almost hear Gerry thinking.) Then, 'Second thoughts, I think I'll use my marmalade glaze as usual,' she said – and laughed until she cried.

A good egg. So I tell myself.

'There was no sign of you,' Pauline says now, her usual theatrical style, 'and the moments ticking by, and the fear clutching my heart, and worse,' and here she pauses and signals elaborately to Alex who has appeared as if by magic, like Mr Benn, 'I was thinking you'd arrive drunk and throw up in my new hall. But you won't do that, darling boys, will you?'

'It's not a thing I've ever done,' I tell her, 'and I won't be starting tonight on a habit like that.'

Alex takes our coats – this the reason for the rapid signalling – and melts away. We murmur, 'Thank you, Alex.'

Pauline resumes.

'And I thought, "what could be keeping them?" I said,' she says, she's really pushing her Galway accent tonight, '"Jesus, Mary, and Joseph," I said, "what could be keeping them?" Didn't I, Alex?' – for Alex has reappeared and now he's carrying a glossily black-lacquered tray on which cluster flutes of prosecco. A very major domo. 'Thank you, Alex,' and I take a glass. Alex is behaving and is being treated like a servant: not least by me, and I think I ought to toss him a coin.

'You forget it takes my husband here three mortal hours to dress himself,' Gerry is saying, simultaneously taking a glass and smiling at Alex, but Pauline is paying no attention, is already leading the way along the narrow, yellow-painted hall and into the thronged sitting room. Yellow in the hall, but the walls in here are of a blue so dark as almost to absorb if not quite disguise the throng of black- and navy-clad men and women sitting and standing and drinking and shouting. 'Inchyra blue,' Pauline says over her shoulder. 'Isn't it the best? Look at me,' she says, 'look at me, against my Inchyra blue walls.'

And now what?

I take a breath.

Well, now to mingle. We're here until midnight at least, aren't we – and Gerry can't slope off. New Year's Eve is the one night in the year when excuses and early departures are impermissible.

They're usually permissible. I know Gerry is 'odd' in the eyes of many, of most of my old crowd. He slips away early, pleading this or that excuse – or worst of all, he doesn't go in the first place, says he doesn't feel up to it.

Are you sure?

Or, a touch of passive aggression: *it'd be more fun if you came too.*

This tendency towards passive aggression is something I have to work on, Gerry says, and again he's right.

Yet again, Alex appears.

'So, Brian, Pauline tells me you're just back from New Zealand. I know it was work, but *lucky beggar*, I said. Is it the erosion, isn't that what you said?'

I did mention erosion to him once – and that's a depressing take-away from a conversation with me. But it's true, I've been studying braided rivers these last several years, and now I say a little bit, or a little bit more (I hope it wasn't too much) about braided rivers, and Alex smiles and encourages, and seems dutiful and even kind, and Pauline passes back and forth, a-sail like the *Queen Mary*.

Just a little bit about braided rivers: because I could go on excessively, I have to watch myself. I like to imagine a picture forming when I'm talking – I mean, in lectures. I like to think about suspension: I like to imagine my words as the soil and sediment washed from the mountain slopes to hang suspended in my braided rivers. 'These rivers, you know, they can be turquoise in colour,' I say to polite Alex, 'like the Rakaia I was studying in New Zealand,' and I see again the waters splitting and now coiling and braiding in their bed, and rolling towards the Pacific.

Making and remaking the land, I could say, and they'll still be here, these rivers, when we're long gone, do you see?

That's the point, I could say. We're talking about another sort of time and history. The future will be different for these rivers, I could say; and I could say that the past was different too.

And this idea of time made and remade, it takes my breath away.

But of course I know not to kid myself, because these words of mine hold nothing suspended – not tonight, anyway. They say that geographers are the boring ones, that geography has no poetry, but that's not the case. It's more that language can't do justice.

Best to say little, or nothing at all, I sometimes think. But, 'That's rubbish,' Gerry has told me. 'That's your problem, my lovely boy, right there.'

'Turquoise,' Alex says now, and he sounds sincere. 'That sounds amazing.'

'To be sure,' Pauline says, and she gestures at the platter of potatoes, sprinkled with what I will later discover is za'atar. She doesn't clap her hands for attention, but she might as well do. 'Everybody, there's plenty more.' She looks across the potatoes and za'atar at me, and for a moment I think she is about to complain publicly about Gerry, about Gerry's unclubbable behaviour: for there Gerry is, washed up in a corner, hoofing into the potatoes. Or that she has someone for me – 'someone I'm dying for you'– to meet. This might be another academic, a bird of a feather with whom I'll be expected to have something or many things in common. Teaching strategies, or research strategies. Or it might be another gay person, with whom I can commune, in gayness or gayhood. 'But I have a husband for that,' I like to imagine myself replying, my patience with Pauline stretched like a rubber band, 'for communing.' But no, it's because the music has shuffled up David Gray, as a monument to our youth, now lost and gone forever, and we look for an instant at one another, across the potatoes.

'Leave me alone,' I want to say to her, or maybe it's 'leave it alone, just leave it,' for already I've noted the ghost or semblance of the younger woman accompanying her tonight, something in the tilt of her chin, the light in her eye that pulls me back to another framing, another poised moment. The music, and walls that are not now blue but stark and white, and there's Dublin just beyond the window.

This year's love had better last, Heaven knows it's high time.

I've been wanting to call it a night, but now I see suddenly that Pauline has other ideas: she doesn't trill that the night is young because she doesn't have to; the sparkle in her eye tells the story. And anyway, I'm not stupid: the atmosphere in the flat has moved up through the gears just in these last minutes: hash, and dreamy laughter and a state approaching somnolence – I hoped – now transforming inexorably into something else. The crowd will move on, go out, no tapering off possible now. Instead, it's clubbing, inexorable: I've been yawning, thinking of Donal and bed, and hoping that Pauline will fall off a cliff as she sometimes does, will vanish to bed, that the crowd cannot fail to get the message, that they'll leave. But no such luck: Pauline is the hostess with the mostest tonight, and Pauline is moving on too. And sure enough:

'Let's go out,' and brooking no opposition, 'we can get a couple of taxis on Baggot Street, and head into town.'

Across the room, Donal – yawning too just a couple of minutes previously – sits up and smiles, glances at me with mingled mischief and sympathy.

'Leave it alone, just leave it,' I want to say.

And of course no surprise, none at all. For these last few weeks, Pauline has been all about Pauline and Pauline's agenda, even more than usual. She's recently met up again with some old flame from Galway – Cyril is this fellow's name, 'Cyrils are common enough in the west, you'd be surprised,' she said – and has brought him home; and as if this isn't enough, has had sex with him in our building's antiquated lift. Donal says that the lift was surely designed expressly for sex: a dark carpet on the walls, a mirror on the ceiling, smoky lighting, and its inner door can be slid open – and on this occasion Pauline did indeed slide it open – to stop the lift moving between floors.

'We'll have to try it ourselves, Brian, so,' Donal said, 'and sure, doesn't dark hides the stains'; and Pauline laughed. I tried to shut her up, or down, by mentioning her Galway convent school, but she only laughed again, and Cyril sniggered, and so I said, 'Speaking of, Cyril, did you know that Pauline's mammy used to collect her and her friends from school and they'd have to say the Rosary right there in the car on the way home? It's true.'

Donal said, 'There's street cred for you, Pauline, you must have been the trendy girl at school, were you?'

Pauline laughed once more. 'I'm not saying the Rosary much these days, is a fact.'

'Shameless hussy,' I said.

'But there's no need for shame,' she said, 'which is a lesson you might learn yourself, Brian,' and so I was the one who was shut up, or down.

And tonight she's in form, she has an agenda, her expression says it all. I watch and Donal turns to her and says, 'I suppose you're after a bit of carpet burn again tonight, Pauline, you have the look of a girl who is,' and Pauline shakes out her hair, and doesn't deny it, and she turns to the stereo and snaps off David Gray, and 'Right, lads.'

There were swans on the canal at Baggot Street Bridge, I remember: white floating on black, and white behind black, where the water falls over the lock. We stop to look over the granite parapet of the bridge, and Donal takes my hand in the darkness – surreptitiously, he knows what I'm like in public; the others are receding, hallooing for non-existent taxis. 'We'll not stay long,' Donal says, 'just a bit of a laugh and then home again.' It's the moment for a kiss, but of course there's no kiss, and then sure enough, a taxi appears, and then another, and all set fair.

Cyril is waiting at the club. He and Pauline have

a way of taking their E that I don't like, that I hate. It is just not classy – so, like Pauline herself. I don't take the stuff myself, of course: it jars with me, the idea that you need to put anything except proper food and drink into your body. Too much butter is the height of my own sin in this regard. And that bloody anxiety from the crowd as each weekend comes around: are the supplies organised, are they all set up, is everything in hand? Then the weekend itself, passing in pouring, flowing sweat, and Sunday to sleep it off. And from Monday the anxiety rising again: are the supplies organised, are they all set up, is everything in hand?

The situation bores me rigid. The whole lot of them do, now.

But I know better than to say so. I know to hold my tongue, let Pauline and Cyril do whatever they want with theirs. 'Least said,' as Donal puts it. 'Let them have their fun.' Surely this phase will pass. Donal himself is less puritanical about the whole thing: he indulges from time to time, though it's a blue moon indulgence; he generally opts out in a way less ostentatious than I can manage. 'Not tonight, for me, I'm grand,' and a laugh to turn the conversation.

Pauline and Cyril, now: the tablet passes from his tongue to her tongue. It definitely isn't convent school behaviour, and I've had words with her about it. 'Would you not wise up a bit,' I've said, and definitely no question mark, 'and stop acting like there's a camera on you the whole time,' at which she'd looked at me as if to say that I didn't know her at all. A camera, a floodlight, a trained pencil spotlight: these are Pauline's accessories of choice.

'Where's your sense of humour? You're boring.'

'No, Pauline, *you're* boring. You just don't realise it,' and she stepped back as though I'd slapped her. She could never be boring.

Tonight, she clearly feels far from boring. She's setting up her ceremony, Cyril is up for it, their tongues are primed and ready. And Donal has caught the atmosphere. 'You don't mind,' he says, and again he touches the inside of my arm, running a forefinger along the soft skin there, our private gesture. 'I want to let off a little steam.'

'I can help, if you need to let off a little steam. All you have to do is ask.'

'But sure we can do that *too*. It's not an either/or situation. Your job is to get me home in one piece.'

And a hesitation, which I remember – but I'm not a party-pooper, I decide, I'm accommodating, I'll keep my judgment to myself, and I say, 'Go on, then. You big eejit.'

Donal laughs at that. Across the table, the ceremony is getting underway; Pauline has already passed a tablet to Donal, and now her tongue and Cyril's tongue are touching and entwining; and the bottles of water are primed, and now Donal pops, and swallows. And later – at sunrise, in hospital – he dies. Bad luck, everyone says, it really was, it must have been a bad tablet, wasn't everyone else grand. I don't go to the hospital, I have no business there; and at the funeral, I sit at the back, in the crowd alongside everyone else.

In the years that follow, Pauline never asks to be forgiven, which means that I never have to explain that I don't forgive her, will not, cannot. Instead, the forgiveness is taken for granted, and its absence is never suspected. Pauline takes much – no, everything for granted; she sails along smooth water, with the picking up of the pieces a job for other people. As for me, I understand something else: that I'm opting to, yes, pick up after her, because this is the easiest choice. The water is smooth, but loaded with sediment, suspended, mucky. It's a piece of good fortune that Pauline leaves for London soon after graduation, in the process shedding Cyril like a piece of litter, while I stay on in Dublin for a year; this gap and space make my choices easier still.

Gerry saw it, more or less at once. 'You like an easy life, don't you? No confrontation.'

I inclined my head, as though to give the comment a measure of respectful attention; then nodded.

'Very true.'

'And what's all that about?'

I shrugged, I spoke some truth. 'Confrontation makes me feel sick.'

Gerry raised an eyebrow. You couldn't go through life without opening up to certain facts, certain situations – so the eyebrow implied. Think about the toxic psychology of it. But my reply would have been, 'I can. Watch me.' And Gerry did, intently, and he mustn't have minded what he saw, because now here we are married, and everything going well enough.

*

'You were having a good old chinwag with patient Alex,' Gerry says in the darkness.

'He was being nice. He was asking me about my rivers.'

'Good man. What did you say?'

'I told him they were turquoise, sometimes. And he seemed to like that idea.'

'Sure, who wouldn't,' Gerry murmurs. 'What else?'

'Go to sleep. Happy New Year.'

'Happy New Year. What else?'

What else. For the last time, as it turns out – though in the moment, I can't know this – I replay the scene with Donal.

'Look, you big eejit. I don't want you to. Let me put my foot down, for Christ's sake.'

'Brian, what else,' Gerry says in the darkness.

'I need to go in the ambulance. He's my boyfriend.'

This is the year of forgiveness, is what I want to say. But this sounds too much like a description of the Chinese New Year – the Year of the Rat, the Year of the Dog, the Year of Forgiveness – so instead, I lie there and Gerry hold me even tighter, and I say, 'I'm going to forgive myself this year.'

'Good man.'

I think: not Pauline, now, and not Donal. I imagine knots coming undone, braids loosening, I imagine a life flowing freely.

'Good man,' Gerry says again. 'And I'll help you. Go to sleep now.'

You Roll
BY JAMES HUDSON

Your name is Tom Carpenter and your name has always
been Tom Carpenter and even when people thought
it was short for Thomas, no, you've always been Tom
Carpenter. The name came from your father, Tom
Carpenter, but you never really leaned into the whole
'Jr.' thing. Him being Tom Carpenter and you being
Tom Carpenter have nothing to do with each other. Not
anymore. Plenty of people have the same name as people
they don't talk to. Take your friend Sissy. You said *"Like
Spacek?"* and she said *"No, like Carrie!"* and then the bass
on a strange Bronski Beat remix shook the club and you
didn't bother talking again until you got to the smoking
area. It turned out her name is Sissy Walsh but she has a
friend called Tom Cruise, no joke. But did you know the
actor's actual real name is Tom Mapother? So really Sissy's
friend Tom Cruise has the cooler moniker. Actually,
her friend Tom Cruise got to pick his name because he's
trans, so it was a real bold move. You never put that much
thought into it. You, you're just Tom Carpenter. For a
while during childhood people called you Tommy but
your dad was never much a fan of that because it made
you sound like a baby, and you were already a big boy of
three years old. He was like, "He's not a fucking *Tommy*,
Deirdre, he's a *Tom*," a firm square Tom. So yeah, the
point being, your name is Tom Carpenter.

Your name is also Tulip Fever, when you can get a gig for her. That doesn't make Tom Carpenter any less your name. You carry your head differently when you're in drag, not just because of the size of some wigs, but you hold your chin up high and your back arched out. Where Tom is concave you, Tulip, no, Tom isn't a separate person, not really. You're concave where you're convex, you're high where you're low, you're long where you're short, you're *extremely* flexible. You can sing, walk, drop, you're beautiful, you have been told by men that you could be a model if you wanted to. You have the legs for it. They tell you so with their hands. You don't look a day over twenty-five, with the right foundation. But you don't want to stand around looking pretty: your drag mother is Scarlet Fever and you love to dance.

Tom and Tulip have coexisted since you were twenty years old and you first met Scarlet Fever on Halloween. You had this tradition at the time, with your little sister Amy, where you would go to the costume store together and pick the worst possible Halloween costumes for each other. You always went kind of easy on Amy since she was your kid sister. Not once did she ever return the favour.

At first you thought Scarlet Fever was a girl, until she admitted to recycling her outfit from an old show. She wouldn't debase herself with store bought Halloween costumes. She scanned you head to toe, from the tube top to the decidedly unshaved legs. She asked, "What are you meant to be?"

You gestured to the pattern on the dress Amy had picked for you, and the fuzzy dice bobbling around your neck. "Sexy Monopoly board."

Does it matter? It matters in the way you have to learn from history, but in the same way, history won't know what to do with you for much longer. What matters is the time-bomb—which is *not* what it sounds like—tucked in your back pocket.

When the stall door is closed in the bathroom of the diner, you take the glowing device out of your pocket and give her a once over. You would have done this at home but your flatmates weren't crazy about the possibility of you turning into the blue guy hanging dong from *Watchmen* so, cool, you'll take your business elsewhere. No ground to argue on anyway, you don't technically live in the apartment, you're Sissy's homeless friend on the couch who works part time at the burger place. Lonnie the manager on the other hand, he was like, "Suit yourself, just do it in the bathroom, don't get so fucked up you can't host drag brunch on Sunday."

"It's not drugs," you said. Lonnie waved his hand. He hired you when you were twenty-nine and the past four years weighed on his back when he just left it at: "Stay safe." It's not that he likes the idea of his employees taking drugs on premises, just that he's no mama bear. He's a shift manager in a novelty burger chain, what can he do.

He can't do what you can do with the time-bomb. The things you'll do to history.

See, it's just, Scarlet Fever had made it look *so easy* to be estranged from your family. She made everything look *easy*, and *fun*, and you don't know how someone could make homelessness look sexy, but it probably had to do with the fact she never called herself 'homeless'. There's something fun and friendly to the words 'crashing on a couch'.

You only noticed that Scarlet's bountiful tips were a benefit of her legacy, not her talents, when you did your first show, and by that time it was a little late for buyer's remorse. You were *out*, come out, kicked out, on the outs, out of luck. A lotta *outta my way kid*. And it's obvious now but you didn't know it at the time, you would have still been you if you weren't *out*. And you only came out because Scarlet was out.

But now the time-bomb looks so snappable in your hands, like it's made of plywood. It's not drugs. It's *not* a bomb. It looks a little like a pregnancy test or a rectal thermometer. It's a little device that you've been told 'explodes time'. The scrap of hand-written instructional paper unfolded from your pocket says this much:

PICK DATE
PUSH BUTTON
GOOD LUCK :)

And there is a dial and a button on the underside of the device. You hadn't noticed them yet. What if you had pressed one by accident? To think you almost butt-dialed a new universe.

Pick date.

Push button.

Unmake one moment from your life.

The options are limited but that means there are still other options than this, though you have spent all the time considering them that you are willing to spend. So many outcomes in life can be decided by the individual person and lucky you, so much of your life has been made by personal choice, but you have never been good at choosing. Life is a series of guesses, educated guesses at best, shots in the dark most nights. Is it wrong to wish someone had forced your hand, so it would have hurt less, so it's not you that fucked everything up?

You've narrowed it down. Not to your two greatest *mistakes*, but two moments that would change the most, if you undid them. When it comes down to it and your thumb is resting on the dial of the time-bomb, you realize you aren't even scared. You aren't looking forward to it either. There's nothing to lose and nothing to gain from changing things, only a lateral move across time. That's probably why fate put this power in your grubby hands. You're just curious enough to use it.

Whatever happens, you hope you will stay yourself in this alternate timeline, or that you will still find yourself again, in time, at a better time, never straying from your true self but just delaying it.

There are two fuzzy dice hanging off your backpack. You prop one on the lid of the toilet and you roll it.

Odds, you don't start doing drag.

Evens, you don't come out to your parents.

You roll.

*

ODDS

Your name is Tom Carpenter and your name has always been Tom Carpenter and even when people thought it was short for Thomas, no, you've always been Tom Carpenter. The name came from your father, Tom

Carpenter Sr., though he hasn't called you Junior in a few weeks. He's just calling you Tom now. You came out to him last month.

Your mother says he doesn't call you Junior because you're a grown man now, but you are thirty-four and you have been grown for a *while*. On the day you came out she put a hand to her chest and said, like she'd been waiting on you to catch up, that in her heart she had always known. The way she talked about it, it felt like everyone knew but they were hoping you wouldn't notice. Your calls home have been thinning since then.

Halloween is coming up, and you're probably going to reuse the Super Mario and Princess Peach costumes with your friend Eddie, because you're both too broke to put a single dollar towards a new costume. It's lazy, but anything other than closet drag is inventive for the kind of gays you hang out with now. A guy throws on a blonde wig and calls it Lady Bunny. Some of the kids say "Trixie Mattel?" and that's when you know you're getting too old for parties this bad. Come the Halloween party, you go for smokes on the balcony with a guy called Tom Cruise, no joke, and he asks if you like Halloween, and you shrug in your plumber's overalls and don't feel strongly about it either way. You've lost track of Eddie and his pink dress. Tom Cruise wants to know if *you'd* be Princess Peach next year and he'll be Mario. "The moustache looks itchy," he says, takes it off your upper lip delicately, and sticks it above his mouth. You've never kissed a man and you think he knows that.

*

EVENS

Your name is Tom Carpenter and your name has always
been Tom Carpenter and even when people thought
it was short for Thomas, no, you've always been Tom
Carpenter. Some people call you Tommy if you and the
other Tom in your friend group are in the same room,
and it feels a little kiddie but you don't hate it. You'd
never introduce yourself as Tommy. You call the other
Tom 'Maverick' because his full name is Tom Cruise,
no joke, and it doesn't catch on, but you like that it's just
between you two.

   Your mom stopped calling you Tommy when you
were a kid, but then started again when you moved out.
That's when your dad stopped caring what she called you,
because you were a grown man and it was out of their
hands. No amount of *Tommy* could make or break a fag
now. This occurs to you in the middle of the night lying
in bed with Maverick. He notices your hand jerk against
his chest and squeezes your shoulders. He asks what's
wrong. You don't know how to explain this conspiracy
of the mind, or if you should even try telling him, you've
just realized your father has disowned you in his heart.
You just tell him you're going home for the weekend and
you're sorry you'll miss drag brunch on Sunday.

   Even though you know the answer, you ask him
is he ever going to come out to his parents, and he says
no, he isn't. Okay. He's three years older than you at
thirty-seven, and you want that to mean he's wiser. It's
not a bad thing, right. He shakes his head. Does he think
his parents know? His mother, yes.

DAYTIME DOGGER
by EMER LYONS

On that Sunday, I learnt my newfound lesbianism had
made me afraid of dicks, in the same way my newfound
sobriety had made me afraid of drink. Everything was
newfound in those days when I was deep in the process
of finding myself after years of falling down every hole,
taking every wrong turn. I'd always had a bad sense of
direction and listened to a podcast once where the woman
on it said she bought a compass and tied it around her
neck. The compass had a smashed face and didn't even
work but she said she felt directed all the same.

It was our first anniversary, and the day was
celebrating as much as we were. Clouds kept themselves
tucked away and everyone smelt like just-bought sun
lotion. We strolled arm in arm, loosely talking of people
we knew and things we wanted from life. The Botanic
Gardens were budding, elderly trees held in place by
complex systems of wire, the roses competing in an age-
old beauty contest, and the cacti choking the air from
our lungs inside their fabricated hot house. You said
you'd never been to the aviary. I led you up the hill, heat
dripping out from under our waistcoats.

The birds were out in force. Sometimes that's not the case, I told you, sometimes they hide. On that day, they'd all come out to show us what they were made of. The macaws sounded like Australia, with the parakeets next door tunnelling for freedom. The cage information said they liked to dig, but I knew the formation of an escape route when I saw one. It was the finches you liked best and I did too with their feathers the colour of a dawn sky rising.

There was something about those public places that you liked; privacy trenched so close to passers-by we'd have to be careful not to be seen. I followed you over tree roots bulging, under stems spiked to press skin to bleed, and lay down next to you when you found the spot where we could hide like the birds on a bad day. You would have been great at guerrilla warfare, there would've been no enemy eyes find you.

I thought I heard someone walk through the grass next to us but tried not to let it distract me from the job at hand. I was leaning on my elbow sideways against you. You were more exposed than I was but then I was better able to see, which turned out to be unfortunate. The grass disrupted again and I slid my hand from your pants to look around. Something ducked behind a nearby tree. You said you'd not seen a thing but then you'd no glasses on. I decided not to let whatever it was bother me thinking it was probably just some bird. It's surprising the racket they can make when they want to. And anyway, you were mad to carry on at that point so there was no stopping.

The next time my peripherals caught the sight of movement, I saw a red head squatted down, peeking through his own glasses, dick in hand, ducking in and out from behind the tree, a bag for life swinging from his dick-free hand as if there wasn't enough going on. I pulled you up with me and led you to the most exposed place in the gardens I could find at speed. You were understandably confused and unsatisfied and wanted to look for somewhere we could finish off. But I couldn't get back in the mood with the thought so fresh in my mind that a man going for a walk after getting groceries on a Sunday lunchtime would stop and start dogging us, it just scandalised me and he didn't even take the time to put his shopping down. Then I suppose he thought himself lucky to find two women with their hands in each other's knickers.

I guess the only man I've ever really known is my father. Growing up, his presence was so big and so small it filled and emptied out the whole house. Sometimes I think I hardly know my mother, even after all we've said to each another over the years. But then we go on mainly about other people and not ourselves, as is the habit of two women talking. Sometimes you and I fell into that habit and after I would feel like a dog who has rolled in something dead, the scent alive and impenetrable.

When I went into work on Monday, I imagined all the fellas in the office wanking under their desks. I imagined that was all they did with their time and that any opportunity that arose to do so they'd take their dick in hand willingly. I thought all fella's wankers and that I was well shot of them.

Months after we stopped having anniversaries and you asked me not to be in the places that you would be, my new girlfriend told me that The Botanic Gardens was notorious for peeping toms as she called them. Turns out not many people in New Zealand are familiar with dogging, even after I tried to explain to them about your man from *Eastenders*. One of the Mitchell Brothers, I would say, never remembering which one. What a dose for the one it wasn't. Apparently, a woman going for a piss was filmed, and other fellas exposed themselves to people ambling round, or maybe it was the same fella every time. Nothing worse than seeing a dick when you least expect it.

I was walking down Princes Street one day, and this fella he comes up to me. He was going on about his flat, and how shit it is, and the holes in the wall, and his landlord not caring about the damp. Seemed pretty standard to me, and your man seemed a bit like a, in my mother's word, down and out. Not that that was any excuse and sure I had lived myself in a place where mushrooms grew in the shower and some days when I was not in the mood for living life to the full, I would think about eating them. I said that to someone else in the house once and she was so shocked I had to pretend I was joking.

Anyway, this fella I keep meeting him, and I see him all around talking to whoever will listen. And sure, isn't it himself! The dogger! I didn't put it together until later, and by then you and I had stopped having anniversaries so I couldn't tell you. I'm starting a new future now with another woman, and I don't know what you are up to but won't we always have this story with the two of us in it to remember that there was a time we couldn't wait to get our hands on each other. Seems strange now with the way you look at me, all full of hate, for what I don't know, even though you did once try to explain to it me. It was too late then for any conversations between us like we were talking different languages without knowing.

I wonder if he knows that I was one of the women that day. Does he get some bang out of having these pure casual conversations with me while we wait for the green man to flash? In the place I live now, there is great water pressure and a cleaner comes in every so often. I still think fondly about the past and you and the mushrooms growing in the shower but I'm not sure I miss any of it.

That Place by the River
by Jamie O'Connell

I was scooping the guts out of a lamb when I heard
Swinger Dingavan was dead. Maureen shouted across
at Steve-o and he knocked off the power hose, the wool
and blood circling around him. She said Swinger was
found in his Golf with a fuckload of drugs down by the
river. A bottle of poppers had rolled in under his seat
and stank the car out.

'At least he died happy. That's more than most
can say.' She had an odd smile on her puss.

I continued dragging out the guts, feeling a bit
sick. I hadn't been mates with Swinger since that night
of the Junior Cert disco fifteen years back. In recent
years, we'd give each other a nod of the head across
McCarthy's. He was a handsome son of a bitch and I'd
often see him scoring the face off a young one in Diceys.

It was the year after the disco that Willie
Dingavan became 'Swinger' Dingavan. The things he
could do with a hurley. That's how he got the name,
though nowadays most folks think he got it from
shagging every young one in Castlemoy. During those
Leaving Cert years they thought he might make the
Cork team, before he went a bit mad. The usual story
where a lad goes off the rails with drink and chasing
women. He got a Civic and Mam, when she heard the
exhaust revving on the street, would shake her head and
say he'd be dead in a ditch before the summer was out.

I think I know why he's really dead. 'Course, I know what killed him, as does the whole fucking town: too much drugs and shite. But that's not a reason. There's always a 'why' and I think it might've all kicked off the night of that disco.

It was me and my sister Aoife's first disco; Mam would never leave us go, not since Billy O'Sullivan got arrested for smacking a Milltown lad after the last one. She said she'd better things to be doing than picking us up from a Garda cell with a shower of other gobshites. Aoife talked Mam round in the end. Mam gave in 'to shut her up'.

'Will Foley be there?' I asked Aoife. I sat on her bed while she got ready. We always got on well, me and Aoife. There's only a year between us.

'Couldn't give a shit,' she said, fiddling with her lashes. She glanced at the stereo, then stared at the door. I knew she was thinking of Mam so I turned the knob. Run DMC was playing.

'Did ye break up?'

'We were only meeting each other. I don't want a boyfriend,' she said. 'Stacey is gonna do slut races. Who you wanna shift?'

'I dunno.' I leaned towards the mirror on Aoife's cupboard, pulling my nose sideways, looking at the bastard of a spot.

'Stop picking. You'll make it worse,' Aoife said. She came over with her makeup thing and rubbed it on my nose. I yanked away. 'Do you want to hide it or what? Stop touching. You'll rub it off.'

I looked in the mirror. It was nearly invisible.

'I bet loads of guys do it,' she said.

Mam dropped us at the hall about eight. There was a row of lads sitting along a wall, drinking from bottles. Aoife's friend Stacey wore a mini skirt and a top that said 'Porn-Star'. Aoife watched Mam drive away.

'Did ya get it?' she asked. Stacey nodded. I followed them around the side. I didn't mind hanging with the girls after being with Aoife at home. I never felt awkward talking to them the way some lads did. Stacey pulled out a bottle of Buckfast. We took turns swigging from it.

'Gimme some.' It was Swinger – Willie as he was known then. I handed him the bottle.

'Your mam okay with me crashing?' I asked. He nodded. We watched a few lads messing with a shopping trolley, pushing each other around the car park. The trolley fell over and they were all laughing. Foley stood up. He slapped a guy on the back. It was Gary Murphy. He'd a face like Plug from *The Bash Street Kids*. He was a lanky fuck, his hair all Brylcreem.

'Do I look okay?' Stacey asked.

'You look amaaazing.' Aoife said. Stacey was chewing her purple lips and half of it was sticking to her teeth. She wasn't a patch on Aoife; you could've driven a truck between her eyes and she'd the brain of a fruit fly.

We polished off the Buckfast before horsing in a few mints, hoping the old guy on the door wouldn't smell the drink. Inside, there was a disco-light that put stars on the ceiling. The gym mats were piled at the far side. A DJ played No Doubt's 'Just a Girl' so loud I could feel the beat in my ribcage. The guys and girls were at either side of the room, so I went with Swinger and Stacy went after Aoife.

'Get your head out of your arse. Do you want your coffee or what?' Maureen shouted across the canteen, holding up the Nescafe tin. I looked back out the window to see if the pigeons were still fighting on the wall.

They'd flown away. I sat down at the table with the lads from my shift. They were all talking about Swinger, hammering on about when they last saw him and 'wasn't it only inevitable'. But none of them talked about where he died. Just as well. Maureen had a smug head on her, telling anyone who'd listen that she worked with Swinger five years back.

'Would you believe, I've been working here the longest,' she said, as if that was something to be proud of. 'Most of ye can't make it past two years.'

She was right. Bit by bit, the stink of dead lambs gets to you. It soaks into your skin and you can't get it off no matter how hard you scrub yourself.

'…It was the stunning that got the better of him,' she said. 'You'd think from the size of him he'd never be such a big girl's blouse.' She laughed and I could see mercury fillings in every one of her teeth.

Stunning: the rows of lambs being pushed one-by-one between railings, having that little metal thing put down on their heads and Swinger pushing the button. There's not many can stick that for long. Not unless they have a taste for it in the first place. When I started, they tried to get me doing it but I said not a hope.

I sometimes wonder if the abattoir is a curse or a blessing for the town. It's handy for lads around here with all the sites closed up. It was the only work I could get after my stint in Australia and I needing to be local since Mam went on chemo. You'd think there'd be more jobs going but an arts degree means fuck all these days.

Melbourne. Now, that's some place. And the beach in St Kilda. Wow. There were some fit looking specimens on it. The ocean was blue like the pictures in magazines. When I was serving pints, I could see it out the window and it'd chill me right out. All that space.

It wasn't just the look of Melbourne that I liked. Down under there was a bit of freedom. You could be anyone. 'Course, I always had to keep an eye out and my heart did jump a few times when I thought I saw someone I knew in Heaven's Door. Most of the crowd in Heaven's Door I wouldn't be able for, too flamboyant for my taste, but there were plenty of normal types too.

I even got to seeing someone in my final few months. Aoife was mad to hear all about it. 'Come on, what are they like?' she'd ask me and I'd be stumped. God only knows if she was doing it to wind me up. She'd settled with her American by then with a second baby on the way. 'Isn't it great to be free of that hole?' she once said to me. 'All those small-minded fucks.' The abuse Mam gave her for getting knocked-up during the Leaving and with Gary fucking Murphy of all people. Poor Sam has those Dumbo ears.

Aoife didn't come home when she heard about the chemo, nor did any of the cousins from England. I'd still five months left on my visa but family was family. Poor Mam was bawling down the phone to me, 'That bitch.'

Coming back to Castlemoy was odd. It's funny how you turn back into your old self again. This place does strange things to the brain. We're all a bit gone in the head from it.

I'm getting away from my point: The Junior Cert disco. If I'm honest, it was a pile of shite. Crap music and all of us glued to the walls.

'I've a naggin in my pants,' Swinger said to me. 'You wanna head to the jacks?'

We jammed into a cubicle and I could feel the heat of his arm touching mine. The whole place stank of piss. The toilet roll had fallen onto the floor and was half-yellow. I swigged the vodka, nearly spitting it up as it burned my throat. It took a few minutes to finish the bottle. My stomach burned. The legs were almost coming out from under me. I leaned my forehead against his shoulder for a second, getting my bearings, and for a few seconds he didn't move.

A few young ones were dancing in the main hall. They thought they were the dog's bollocks, staring at the lads, but none of us left the wall. Then Aoife got up with Stacy and Foley was straight in there. The rest followed. I sat on the ground with Swinger, feeling sick. The room was spinning.

'Stay awake. They'll kick us out.' Swinger gave me a dig. There was a group of adults by the door. I watched the crowd. Stacey was kissing Gary and Aoife was shouting in Foley's ear. It seemed like all the lads wanted the same few girls.

I stood up, my knees just holding. Swinger and I danced with these two from Loretto; he moved towards the blond and they began shifting each other. Her friend was giving me the eye and I was gonna go for it but then I felt sick and had to leg it to the jacks.

I chucked-up into the toilet. It was filthy but I couldn't lift myself off the rim. I closed my eyes, thinking

I should text Aoife but my arms were all weak.

'Hey!' Some tool kicked the door. I woke up, feeling dizzy. I took a deep breath and opened the latch, staggering to the sink. The hot water tap was long gone. I washed my hands with the cold and walked back into the hall, balancing against the wall. I felt better after getting it all up. Swinger was still shifting the blond, well, not so much shifting as eating the face off her. Her friend was mauling the head of some other lad. I played *Snakes* on my phone. The clock was barely moving.

Aoife and Stacey dragged me up to dance. I felt mad awkward at first but then I didn't mind.

'Still with the girls,' Gary shouted over. Aoife flipped him the finger.

The disco finished at eleven thirty, the big lights coming on. Aoife's chin and her nose were pink from all the shifting.

'How many?' she turned to Stacy.

'Five.'

'Ha, seven.'

'D'you think we should find Mam,' I said.

Mam was in the Toyota outside, waiting for Aoife. I straightened up, thinking of the booze I'd drank. Mam asked if we wanted a lift but Swinger shook his head, saying he only lived around the corner. He told her we'd head straight back.

'Make sure you do now,' she said.

It was getting dark when I left the abattoir. I zipped up my hoodie as I walked out the gates, my breath fogging. A few of the lads from the shift were chatting at the entrance. Maureen rubbed her cigarette butt into the pavement and asked me was I going to my Mam's or did I have a date with a girl. She started roaring with that fag-ash laugh you get from being a dried-up bitch who's spent two decades in the pub.

I'd love to tell her and the rest of them where to shove it. Maybe when I get out of this place I will. Anyhow, Maureen's other-half is inside and her sixteen-year-old is fostered, so she's getting her comeuppance either way.

I walked towards the town centre, wondering how much longer I could put up with it all, the blood, the guts and Maureen's sour puss. Then it hit me again what'd happened. Swinger was dead. It seemed mad to me that someone like him, who was all go, could be gone. I wondered how Stacy took the news and if she'd told Swinger's two boys yet. She and Swinger didn't live together or anything; no-one knew if it was because of social welfare or if he'd got kicked out for having a roving eye. However, the two of them seemed happy enough in the pictures I'd seen online.

I flicked open Stacy's profile on my phone. She'd put a photo of Swinger up as her profile pic. I thought again what a handsome fucker he was. My eyes were stinging a fair bit. Fifteen years since we'd talked. It was stupid. I read down through the messages on Stacy's wall – all these folks coming out of the woodwork, offering their condolences but really just having a nose. I saw Maureen's post, 'Thinking of you babes xx'. I stuffed the phone back in my pocket.

Passing Supermacs, I could see one of the girls at the counter. She gave me a wave. I nodded and walked on, down towards the river. Home was only five minutes up the hill after the bridge.

When I reached the bridge, I paused, thinking maybe I'd turn left. About seven or eight minutes up the quays would bring me to where he'd died. Would the red Nissan be there, a bit hidden by the trees? Would that odd guy appear and look about for others? I hoped not. A bit of respect for the dead and all that.

What a godforsaken place. Confused young fellas and married men who should know better, their clueless wives at home watching *Eastenders*. I was embarrassed for Swinger to be with that sad lot. Why did anyone go there? Hadn't they phones and apps to be getting what they wanted?

It's a wonder there's never been a rumour about Swinger in all these years. I suppose anyone else going to that place would hardly be announcing it. To think, Swinger was calling some lad a faggot outside McCarthy's a few weeks back, though maybe I heard wrong. Sometimes, when I pass people on the street, I think I hear them saying 'fag' but maybe they aren't saying anything at all.

After we left the disco, Swinger and I passed by Supermacs. Across the road, a few of the local heads were drinking out the front of Diceys. The cold air brought me around, the vodka wearing off.

'Did you shift anyone?' Swinger asked. His hands were stuffed in his jeans. He shivered.

'Nah. Did you?'

'Just that girl Tracey but for ages.'

'Was she good?'

'She was all right. I felt her tits too.'

'What did they feel like?'

'Kinda small.'

'Oh.'

We stopped in Centra. I picked up a packet of BBQ Beef Hula Hoops and a can of coke. Swinger got four sausage rolls from the deli. After turning off the main street, we came to his house. We were ten minutes late but he said his mam didn't give a shit. I watched the bits of pastry sticking to his lips. He squirted tomato sauce from the packet straight into his mouth.

'Gimme some coke there,' he said. I handed it to him and he took a big swig. When he gave it back, there was food on it but I didn't care.

'Can you smell drink?' he asked. He breathed into my face. It was warm. I could only smell ketchup.

'No, you're grand. What about me?'

'Fuck sake, the bang of Hula Hoops.'

I laughed. Swinger slipped his key into the lock and twisted it real slow.

'We'd better keep it down,' he said. I followed him up the stairs, across the landing to his bedroom, the floorboards creaking. He closed the door and flicked on the light. The room smelt like dirty socks.

'Will, is that you?' a woman's voice shouted through the walls.

'Yes Mam.'

'Get into bed now.'

Swinger stuck up his two fingers at the wall then took off his jersey. He'd a triangle of hair on his chest and around his nipples. I put down my shoes, taking off my jeans. I looked about the room; the football wallpaper was torn around the bed.

'Mind topping and tailing?' he said. 'Mam has the airbed downstairs but fuckit, if we wake her again, she'll blow.'

'Grand,' I said, lying on the mattress. He got out to turn off the light. There was a birthmark on top of his back in the shape of a gun, so he told everyone. Then he jumped in, his feet close to my head. I lay still and wondered if I was taking up too much space. Lying down made the drink worse.

'Fuck, I've a head on me,' he whispered from the other end of the bed.

'Me too,' I said. I licked my teeth, feeling the bits of crisps.

'Fuck,' I yelled. Swinger laughed. He was after punching my foot. I kicked him. He kicked back. I grabbed his leg, smacking my pillow down on his head. He yanked himself free, jumped up and pinned my shoulders down, while I tried to knee him.

'Boys, keep it down. Get some sleep,' his mam shouted. Swinger looked at the wall and I watched the muscle on his neck which went from his ear to his collarbone. He looked back at me and I could see the white of his teeth. He was pushing hard against me. I reached down. I thought he might've punched me but he didn't pull away.

The next morning, Swinger was up before me. I'm not quite sure how he got his arm out from under my neck. My lips felt warm from his stubble. Putting on my clothes, I tried not to think about his lips. When I did, I started getting hard and fuck, that was that last thing I wanted.

On the stairs, I felt sick. What if his mam heard

something? I suppose she'd have been straight into us if she had an inkling.

I could hear the TV going in the sitting room. Swinger was sitting on the floor with the Mega Drive, playing *Streets of Rage*. I sat on the edge of the couch and said good morning but he never turned around. I laughed, saying that the woman with the whip was like Aoife but he never said anything. There wasn't even a chuckle out of him. My cheeks started to feel really hot and I sat back watching Alex Stone kick the shit out of a baddie. Every time I tried to say something, the words got caught in my throat.

Mam picked me up at eleven and I left Swinger playing. He didn't look up the whole time. My head was pounding as I shouted goodbye and closed the door.

Swinger and I barely said a word to each other since then. He got mad into the hurling that autumn and the man known as 'Swinger Dingavan' was born, chasing women and downing pints with the lads. Who knows what he was thinking about all those years, and then to die where he did.

In the end, I didn't turn left up the river but went straight over the bridge and carried on home to Mam. I helped her into bed, then I ordered a Dominos and watched a few episodes of *Family Guy* off the laptop. I guess there's no point in being dramatic about things. What's done is done. You've just got to get on with it.

Sleep
by Colm Tóibín

I know what you will do when morning comes. I wake
before you do and I lie still. Sometimes I doze, but usually
I am alert, with my eyes open. I don't move. I don't want
to disturb you. I can hear your soft, calm breathing and
I like that. And then at a certain point you turn toward
me without opening your eyes; your hand reaches over,
and you touch my shoulder or my back. And then all
of you comes close to me. It is as though you were still
sleeping—there is no sound from you, just a need, almost
urgent but unconscious, to be close to someone. This is
how the day begins when you are with me.

It is strange how much unwitting effort it has
taken to bring us here. The engineers and software
designers could never have guessed, as they laid out their
strategies and sought investment, that the thing they
were making—the Internet—would cause two strangers
to meet and then, after a time, to lie in the half-light of
morning, holding each other. Were it not for them, we
would never have been together in this place.

One day you ask me if I hate the British, and I say that I do not. All that is over now. It is easy to be Irish these days. Easier maybe than being Jewish and knowing, as you do, that your great-aunts and uncles perished at Hitler's hands. And that your grandparents, whom you love and visit sometimes out on Long Island, lost their brothers and sisters; they live with that catastrophe day in, day out.

It is a pity that there is such great German music, you say, and I tell you that Germany comes in many guises, and you shrug and say, "Not for us."

We are in New York, on the Upper West Side, and when I open the blinds in the bedroom we can see the river and the George Washington Bridge. You don't know, because I will never tell you, how much it frightens me that the bridge is so close and in full view. You know more about music than I do, but I have read books that you have not read. I hope that you will never stumble on a copy of James Baldwin's *Another Country*; I hope that I will never come into the room and find you reading it, following Rufus through New York to his final journey up this way, on the train, to the bridge, the jump, the water.

There is a year missing in your stories of your life, and this makes everyone who loves you watch you with care. I have asked you about it a few times and seen your hunched shoulders and your vague, empty look, the nerdy look that you have when you are low. I know your parents dislike the fact that I am older than you, but the knowledge that I don't drink alcohol or take drugs almost makes up for that, or I like to think it does. You don't drink or take drugs, either, but you do go outside to smoke, and maybe I should take up smoking, too, so that I can watch over you casually when you are out there and not have to wait and then feel relief when I hear the doors of the elevator opening and your key in the lock.

There is no year in my life that I cannot account for, but there are years that I do not think about now, years that went by slowly, in a sort of coiled pain. I have never bothered you with the details. You think I am strong because I am older, and maybe that is the way things should be.

I am old enough to remember when things were different. But no one cares now, in this apartment building or in the world outside, that we are men and we wake often in the same bed. No one cares now that when we touch each other's face we find that we both need to shave. Or that when I touch your body I find a body like mine, though in better shape and twenty and more years younger. You are circumcised and I am not. That is a difference. We are cut and uncut, as they say in this country where we both live now, where you were born.

Germany, Ireland, the Internet, gay rights, Judaism, Catholicism: they have all brought us here. To this room, to this bed in America. How easy it would have been for this never to have happened. How unlikely it would have seemed in the past.

I feel happy, rested, ready for the day as I return from the shower and find you lying on your back with your glasses on, your hands behind your head.

"You know that you were groaning in the night? Almost crying. Saying things." Your voice is accusing; there is a quaver in it.

"I don't remember anything. That's funny. Was it loud?"

"It was loud. Not all the time, but just before the end it was loud, and you were waving your hands around. I moved over to you and whispered to you, and then you fell back asleep. You were all right then."

"When you whispered to me, what did you say?"

"I said that it was all OK, that there was nothing wrong. Something like that."

"I hope I didn't keep you awake."

"It was no problem. I went back to sleep. I don't know what you were dreaming about, but it wasn't good."

The fear comes on Saturdays, and it comes, too, if I am staying somewhere, in a hotel room, for example, and there is shouting in the street in the night. Shouting under my window. I keep it to myself, the fear, and by doing this sometimes I keep it away, at arm's length, elsewhere. But there are other times when it breaks through, something close to dread, as though what happened had not occurred yet but will occur, is about to do so, and there is nothing I can do to stop it. The fear can come from nowhere. I may be reading, as I often do on Saturdays while you practice or go to a concert with your friends. I am reading and then suddenly I look up, disturbed.

The fear enters the pit of my stomach and the base of my neck like pain, and it seems as if nothing could lift it. Eventually, as it came, it will go, though not easily. Sometimes a sigh, or a walk to the fridge, or making myself busy putting clothes or papers away, will rid me of it, but it is always hard to tell what will work. The fear could stay for a while, or come back as though it had forgotten something. It is not under my control.

I know where I was and what I was doing when my brother died. I was in Brighton, in England, and I was in bed and I could not sleep, because there were drunken crowds shouting below my hotel window. Sometime between two and three in the morning he died, in his own house in Dublin. He was alone there that night. If I had been sleeping at the moment when it happened, I might have woken, or at least stirred in the night. But probably not. Probably I would just have gone on sleeping.

He died. That is the most important thing to say. My brother was in his own house in Dublin. He was alone. It was a Saturday night, Sunday morning. He called for an ambulance before two in the morning. When it arrived, he was dead, and the paramedics could not bring him back to life.

I have never told anyone that I was awake in that room in Brighton in those hours. It hardly matters. It matters only to me and only at times.

On one of those winter evenings when you are staying here, we go to bed early. Like a good American, you wear a T-shirt and boxers in bed. I am wearing pyjamas, like a good Irishman. Chet Baker is on low. We are both reading, but I know you are restless. Because you are young, I always suspect that you are horny when I am not, and that is a joke between us. But it is probably true; it would make sense. In any case, you move toward me. I have learned always to pay attention when this happens, never to seem distracted or tired or bored. As we lie together, you whisper.

"I told my analyst about you."

"What about me?"

"About your crying in the night and my coming home on Saturday to find you looking so frightened or sad or something that you could barely talk."

"You didn't say anything about it on Saturday. Was it this Saturday?"

"Yeah, it was Saturday. I didn't want to raise the subject."

"What did he say?"

"He says that you have to do something about it. I told him you said that Irish people don't go to analysts."

"What did he say?"

"He said that explains why there are so many bad Irish novels and plays."

"There are some good Irish plays."

"He doesn't think so."

We lie there listening to Chet Baker singing "Almost Blue," and I move to kiss you. You prop yourself up on your elbow and look at me.

"He says that you have to get help but it has to be Irish help, only an Irish analyst could make sense of you. I told him that you didn't hate the British, and maybe you could get, like, a British one, and he said it sounded like you needed help even more urgently than he'd thought."

"Do you pay him for this rubbish?"

"My dad pays him."

"He sounds like a bundle of laughs, your shrink."

"He told me not to listen to you. Just to make you do it. I said that you were OK most of the time. But I've told him that before. Hey, he likes the sound of you."

"Fuck him!"

"He's good, he's nice, he's smart. And he's straight, so you don't have to worry about him."

"That's true. I don't have to worry about him."

Spring comes, and something that I had forgotten about begins. Behind this apartment building is an alley, or an opening between two buildings, and if it is warm at night some students gather there, maybe the ones who smoke. Sometimes I hear them and the sound becomes part of the night, like the noise the radiators make, until it fades. It has never bothered me in all the time I have lived here, and I have no memory of your ever remarking on it. It is quiet here, quiet compared with downtown or the apartment you share in Williamsburg on the nights when you do not stay with me.

Nonetheless, I should have known that some night that noise would find me in my sleep. Maybe if I had got an Irish shrink, as your shrink suggested, he would have warned me about this, or I would have come to warn myself after many meetings with him.

I don't remember how it begins, but you do. I am whimpering in my sleep, or so you say, and then going quiet for a while. And then when there is more shouting in the alley behind the building I start to shiver. You say that it is more like someone shuddering, recoiling in fright, but still I have no memory of this. When you try and fail to wake me, you become afraid. I know that everything you do, the way you manage your day, is driven by your need never to become afraid.

When I finally wake, you are on your cell phone and you look frightened. You tell me what happened and then you reach for your shirt.

"I'm going."

"What's wrong?"

"I'll talk to you in the morning. I'm going to get a cab."

"A cab?"

"Yeah, I have money."

I watch you dress. You are silent and deliberate. Suddenly, you seem much older. In the light from the lamp on your side of the bed I can see what you will look like in the future. You turn as you go out the door.

"I'll text."

Within a minute you are gone. It is three-forty-five when I look at the clock. When I text and say that I am sorry for waking you, you do not reply.

The next evening you come over. I can tell that you have something to say. You ignore me when I ask if you have eaten.

"Hey, I'm going to take my clothes and stuff."

"I'm sorry about last night."

"You scared me. There's something wrong with you. I don't know what it is, but it's too much for me."

"You don't want to stay here again?"

"Hey, I never said that. That is not what I said."

You sigh and sit down. I start to talk.

"Maybe we should—"

"No, no 'maybe,' and no 'we should.' You have to go and see someone. You can't do this on your own, and I can't help you, and I'm not staying here again until you've done that. It's not because I don't want to, but it's weird. It wasn't just once, just one bad dream. It's intense. You should hear it. I thought I should record it on my phone for you, so you would know."

I imagine you holding the phone out in the dark with the RECORD button on while I am having a bad

111

dream I can't wake from.

"Why don't we talk during the week?"

"Sure."

You go to the bedroom and after some minutes reappear with a bag.

"Are you certain you want to take your stuff?"

"Yeah."

You have already taken the keys to this apartment off your key ring and you put them on the hall table. We hug and you leave with your head down. I stand with my back to the door and my eyes closed as I hear the elevator arrive and open its doors for you. And all I can think is that I would never have done this to you, walked out like that. And all I can think then is that maybe that's what's wrong with me. You have learned something that I don't want to know.

There is always that sense of being released when the plane takes off from J.F.K. to Dublin. Every Irish person who gets on that plane knows the feeling; some, like me, also know that it does not last for long. I read a bit and then sleep and then wake up and look around and go to the bathroom and notice that most of the other passengers are sleeping. But I don't think I will sleep again. I don't want to read. There are almost four hours still to go.

I doze and wake and then fall into the deepest sleep in the hour before we land, so that I have to be woken and told to put my seat in the upright position.

There is a hotel on St. Stephen's Green, on the opposite side from the Shelbourne, and I have booked a room there for four nights. I have told no one that I am coming here, except the doctor, a psychiatrist, whom

I met years ago, when he helped a friend of mine who was suffering from depression and could not sleep and could not handle anything. The doctor knew my friend's family. I remember the time he spent with my friend and how he came back again and again. His kindness, his patience, his watchfulness. I remember that I made him tea on a few of those nights, and we spoke about the late Beethoven quartets and he told me which recordings he favored, as my friend lay next door in a darkened room. I remember that he liked jazz and that he found it strange that I did not.

Until I met you, that is. I liked listening to jazz with you.

When I called him from New York, he remembered that time and mentioned also that he had read a few of my books. He said that he would see me, but it would be best not to do it when I was jet-lagged. He told me to take a few days between landing in Dublin and the appointment. He was living alone now, he said, so he could see me at his house. He gave me the address, and we agreed on the time. When I asked about payment, he told me I could send him some jazz CDs from New York or my next book.

In Dublin, I keep to the side streets on the first day. I go to the cinema in the afternoon and then up into Rathmines and find a few places to linger, where I think I will meet no one I know. The city seems low-key, almost calm.

There is a new cinema in Smithfield and I go there on the second day and see two films in a row. I find a place to eat nearby. I notice how crowded it becomes, and how loud the voices are, how much laughing and shouting there is. I think about the city I used to know, which was a place that specialized in the half-said thing, the shrug, a place where people looked at one another out of the corner of their eye. All that is over now, or at least in Smithfield it is.

I try not to sleep during the daytime on either of those days, although I want to. I go to Hodges Figgis and Books Upstairs and buy some books. In the evening, I watch the Irish news and some current-affairs programmes on the television in my hotel room.

And then on the third day, in the late afternoon, I go to Ranelagh to see the psychiatrist. I am unsure what we will say or do. I am scheduled to go back to New York the following day. Maybe there is a drug for what is wrong with me, but I doubt it. I need him to listen to me, or maybe I just need to be able to tell you when I come back that I have done this. Maybe, I think, he will refer me to someone in New York whom I can see in the same regular way that you see your analyst, as you call him.

There is a long room that was once two rooms, and it is beautifully furnished. We take our shoes off and sit opposite each other on armchairs toward the back of that room. I realize that he does not need me to talk; he listened carefully to what I said on the phone. He asks me if I have ever been hypnotized, and I say no. There was a guy, I remember, who used to do it on television or in the theatre. I can't recall his name—Paul something— but I have seen him on television once or twice. I think of hypnosis as a party game, or something that happens in black-and-white films. I did not expect the psychiatrist to suggest it as something he might do with me.

He is, he says, going to use hypnosis. We will both need to be quiet. It would be best if I closed my eyes, he says. I think for a second that I should ask him why he is doing this, or whether he does it all the time, or what it could achieve, but there is something about the calm way that he approaches the task, something deliberate, that makes me feel that it is better not to ask anything. I am still wary and I am sure he notices this, but it does not deter him. I close my eyes.

He leaves silence. I don't know for how long he leaves silence. And then in a new voice, a voice that is more than a whisper but still has an undertow of whispering, he tells me that he is going to count to ten, and at the word "ten" I will be asleep. I nod and he begins.

His voice has a softness but also an authority. I wonder if he has trained in hypnosis or if he developed his method on his own with other patients. When he gets to "ten," there is no great change. But I do not move or tell him that I am still awake. I keep my eyes closed, trying to guess how long it will be before he realizes that the spell has not worked, that I am not asleep, that I still know where I am.

"I want you to think about your brother."

"I'm getting nothing."

"I want you to take your time."

I leave my mind empty and my eyes closed. Nothing is happening, but there is a density to the feelings I am having, although the feelings themselves are ordinary ones. I am oddly relaxed and also uneasy. It is like a moment from childhood, or even adulthood, in which I am able to stop worrying about a pressing matter for a moment in the full knowledge that the worry will come back. During this interlude I do not move or speak.

"I want you to think about your brother," he says again.

I let out a small moan, a sort of cry, but there is no emotion behind it. It is as if I were just doing what he expects me to do.

"Nothing, nothing," I whisper.

"Follow it now."

"There's nothing."

He leaves silence, leaves space for me to moan and tell him where I am going, but I am not sure where that is. It seems like nowhere in particular. I am moving. I am also awake. He speaks several times more, his voice softer and more insistent. And then I stop him. I need silence now and he leaves silence again. I sigh. I am puzzled. I cannot tell where I am going. I know that I am sitting in an armchair in a house in Ranelagh and that I can open my eyes at any moment. I know that I am going back to New York tomorrow.

And then it comes, the hallway, and it is a precise hallway in a house I have known but never lived in. There is lino on the floor and a hall table and a door to a living room, the door slightly ajar. There are stairs at the end of the hallway.

And then there is no "I." I am a "he." I am not myself.

"Do you feel sad about your brother?" the psychiatrist asks.

"No. No."

I am lying on the floor of that hallway. I am dying. I have called an ambulance and left the front door on the latch.

The dying comes as lightness, a growing lightness, as though something were leaving me, and I am letting it leave, and then I am panicking, or almost panicking, and then feeling tired.

"Follow how you feel."

I signal for him not to speak again. The idea that there is less of me now, and that this lessness will go on and there will be even less of me soon, that this diminishment will continue, is centered in my chest. Something is going down, going out, with a strange and persistent ease. There is no pain, more a mild pressure within the self, or the self that I am now, in this hallway, this room. It is happening within the body as much as within the self that can think or remember. Something is reaching out to death, but it is not death; "death" is too simple a word. It is closer to an emptying out of strain, until all that is left is nothing—not peace or anything like that, just nothing. This is coming gradually and inevitably. I, we, are smiling, or seem to be content and have no concerns. It is almost pleasure, but not exactly pleasure, and not exactly the absence of pain, either. It is nothing, and the nothing comes with no force, just a desire or a need, which seems natural, to allow things to proceed, not to get in their way.

I think then that the experience is ending, and before it does I want to know if our mother is close now, but that comes as a question only. I see her face, but I do not feel her presence. I hold the thought and find myself longing for some completion of it, some further satisfying image, but nothing comes. Instead, there is stillness, and then the sound of the door being pushed open and voices. I can hear their urgency, but it is like urgency in a film that I cannot fully see; it is not real. It is in the background as I am lifted, as my chest is pushed and pummelled, as more voices are raised, as I am moved.

Then there is nothing, really nothing—the nothing that I am and the nothing that is in this room now. Whatever has happened, it has ended. There is nowhere else to go.

I begin to moan again, and then I am quiet and stay quiet until the psychiatrist says softly that he will count to ten again, and when he says the word "ten" I will come back from where I have been and I will be in the room with him.

"I don't know where you were, but I left you there."

I do not reply.

"Maybe you got something you can work on."

"I became him."

"Did you feel sad?"

"I was him. I wasn't me."

He looks at me calmly.

"Maybe the feelings will come now."

"I became him."

We do not speak for a while. When I look at my watch I think that I am misreading it. The watch says that two hours have passed. It is almost dark outside. He makes tea and puts on some music. When I find my shoes, I discover that I have trouble putting them on, as if my feet had swelled during the time that I was elsewhere. Eventually, I stand up and prepare to leave. He gives me a number I can call in a few weeks when I have absorbed what happened.

"What *did* happen?" I ask.

"I don't know. You are the one who has to do

the work."

He follows me in his stocking feet to the front door. We shake hands, and I leave. I walk through Dublin, from Ranelagh to St. Stephen's Green, passing people on their way home from work.

It is winter in New York and I have not replied to your texts. They come more sporadically and say less and less. It is down to "Hey!" or "Hi" and soon, I think, they will stop. When I go to Lincoln Center to see a film or hear music, I look at the list of upcoming concerts and check to see if your name is there. It would not surprise me on one of those nights if I found you standing close by, looking at me.

I wake alone now. I wake early and lie thinking or dozing. In the morning, I carry the full burden of the night's sleep. It is as if I had been tiring myself out in the darkness, rather than resting. There is no one to tell me if I make a sound as I sleep. I don't know if I snore, or whimper, or cry out. I like to think that I am silent, but how can I tell?

VISUAL SNOW
BY DECLAN TOOHEY

1

When we met, Andrew Ward lived under absurd conditions.

Absurd, that is, because his mornings and nights, his evenings and afternoons, in short the gamut of his waking seconds, revolved around a literary project into which he had already thrown three dogged years of work and for which, regrettably, he would receive in his life neither a morsel of recognition nor a scrap of acclaim.

I speak, of course, of Ward's doctoral thesis, which at the time I entered Maynooth, as an aloof yet gullible undergraduate, he said he'd complete in approximately six months. About this he turned out to be wrong.

Still, it was quite the sight to see, Ward's library grind. The horrific posture and sunken pose. The scowl in his usual seat. The tower of books by or about Thomas Mann. His HP Pavilion g6, whirring away at a distracting and chronic volume.

On what precise topic he'd proposed to whack out approximately 80,000 words I can never remember. I'm sure he informed us the morning of that infamous first seminar; something, maybe, about embryonic issues within the field of ecocriticism, and how they play out in *The Magic Mountain* or *Buddenbrooks*.

Regardless, that semester would be Andrew's last, not for anything to do with the submission of his thesis or the completion of his *viva*—he would never get around to either—but because, in a tragic turn of events, on Christmas Eve of all blasted days, the wretched sod went missing and was never seen again.

2

But that's beside the point. Our introductory seminar was where I first thought that, through him, I might learn a smidgen about love, or what love actually was.

Less a classroom than a spacious dressing cubicle, Room 1.3 of Maynooth's Iontas Building was a contender for the most inhospitable seminar room in all of Ireland.

This mostly had to do with the begrudging fact that only fifteen chairs comfortably fit around the room's oval table, and yet the beginning of every academic year saw at least twenty-three students in each EN151 seminar. Those who weren't early enough to secure a prime spot were obliged to choose from the seats by the walls—on chairs whose plastic swivel rests made one feel imprisoned and on which to take legible notes was a task fit for Job.

Adding further ergonomic insult to injury, the room boasted the university's sole set of sentient windows, opening and closing to suit their whims no matter the weather outside, no matter the energy one exerted in foostering around with their paired remote. They could not be persuaded, these sentient windows;

like time and tide they heeded no man. And invariably they operated on a temperature system at odds with ours: when we were so hot as to be falling asleep they refused to open, and when the exterior chill rendered it impossible to concentrate they declined to close.

The first Tuesday it was stuffy, mainly because of the Indian summer in whose throes we remained ensnared. All twenty-three of us were seated. My notebook lay upon the table and my blue BIC biro—the sole pen with which I've permitted myself to write in the past decade, since I promised myself at the age of sixteen never to use an Aldi or a Lidl or a Eurostore biro again— rested behind my ear.

The table-dwelling patricians and the backseat plebeians made three equal groups: those with laptops, those with pen and paper, and those with nothing save for the boon of their presence. I looked upon everyone, irrespective of their equipment, and inwardly swore to out-grade them all. Those who didn't belong here; those disinterested and apathetic; those who'd learn but the essentials of acadamese in order to advance their teacherly ambitions; those rare few whom I considered my rivals— no one was safe from the wrath of my writerly conquest.

Not even Ward, whose smile was calculated, his coat a camelhair tan. Thanks to the proficiency of my detective skills, I perceived in his voice the clear timbre of an English accent, though on account of my egregious knowledge of British geography I was unable to determine the particulars of his provenance. His demeanour recalled that of a spy or a pantomime villain; an unusual thought since I hated pantomimes and knew next to nothing about spies. I had left the last Bond movie so bored that I swore never to watch another again—a vow to which I have since remained faithful.

'Welcome,' said Ward, his palms opening outward in greeting. 'Over the next twelve weeks you will all become very sick.'

Mine could not have been the only eyebrow to arch, nor forehead to tighten, at that exact moment in Iontas's R1.3.

'Sick, that is, of William Wordsworth, his poetry, daffodils, iambic tetrameter, and manifold forms of literary criticism. Notwithstanding this biblio-illness you'll all incur, I *hope* we'll have some interesting discussions. I hope I won't have to do all the talking, and that you'll each be as garrulous as the other. My aim is to provide the fodder, if you will, so that you might be the cannons; though I'm aware, given how green—sorry, that's presumptuous of me to say... given how *new* some of you are to the game, is what I meant... this might be a lot to ask.'

The windows creaked open.

'If however, at the end of the semester, you take nothing away from these tutorials save for a *solid* grasp of literary criticism's most prevalent methodologies—what they are and how to use them—then that, truly, is all I can ask for. That would be, in a word, just splendid.'

While I abstained from observing out loud that he had just used two words, my appearance must have displayed some tell-tale tic, for upon my face then fell Ward's feline eyes, one of which, for reasons I will never be able to verify, had the gall, the *mettle*, to wink overtly in my specific direction.

3

Now, before we proceed any further, I must address the
mammoth in the vestibule.

My actions that semester were not contrived. Nor
were they emblematic of the kind of masculine crisis with
which, I'm guessing, the average person is most familiar:
namely, exuberant displays of macho braggadocio that
seek to compensate for a man's homosexuality.

Let me be frank.

Despite my relative youth, I have had many
relationships with men and women—and have always
been open about that. For me sexuality is a topic into
which we should always be willing to hurl ourselves, or
around which there should be the option, at any time,
of an open discussion. Moreover, I see it as a mere
appendage; sexuality does not determine my being, my
sense of self, my place in the world, or anything else. It's
just there. (There are, granted—and rightfully so—those
for whom the opposite is true. More power to them.)

In other words: Ward and I had sex. Once.
Terribly.

But during those months I had numerous sexual
partners, and though none are particularly memorable,
my time with Ward sticks out above the rest. You see,
for the past eleven years I've had a cunt of a problem:
depersonalisation. I experience emotions at one remove,
feel profoundly disconnected from reality, and perceive
at all times faint floating objects which dance before
my eyes like snowflakes. My hands belong to somebody
else; for vision I'm either far back in my head or floating
outside my body. None of these are pleasurable. Since

I ate an ounce of weed more than a decade ago and, in doing so, acquired my disorder, love has never been something of which I've felt capable.

Yet Ward was peculiar. For him I didn't *care*. With him I wasn't *infatuated*. Whatever he made me feel, it was something more complex than fuck-hungry desire.

That much was clear, I think, from the moment he encouraged us to verbally abuse each other in class.

4

All too aware of the first-year undergrad's propensity for shyness, if not classroom-conditional bouts of inhibition, Ward believed in a catalyst that would loosen the most taciturn of students, so that they could freely pontificate upon any literary or theoretical topic at hand. This spark, surprisingly, was not kindled by an academic superior, but instead took the form of decidedly personal comments from the student's own peers.

He called this stimulus Wardian conditioning.

And if that morning's tutorial was anything to go by, it produced in part the desired effect—only Ward had wanted his students to hold forth on the sophistications of nineteenth-century poetry, not to threaten each other with such voluble hostility that he would give momentary thought to calling someone, *anyone*, of greater presence than himself to extinguish the inferno he'd took pains to ignite.

But what stood out for me the most, among the catcalls and snarls, wasn't just that Ward's brain was something I wished to know better, to get inside of and rummage around; it was also the precision and lucidity of Maebh Kealy's words, which came forth, funnily enough, at the apogee of the world's single session of Wardian conditioning.

She said that Wordsworth anticipated the fall of man, by which she meant the death of traditional masculinity, by which she meant, furthermore, the demise of masculinity as a hegemonic structure. She said that masculinity, today, is a vehicle through which one successfully advances a capitalist agenda, irrespective of one's gender, and that Wordsworth's daffodils are indicative of what was, strictly speaking, a twenty-first-century condition.

Ward was ecstatic—it seemed his ploy was working. How Maebh arrived at this thesis was beyond me. But as I looked out the window and reflected further on her words, I caught a glimpse of what I'd understand later that semester: that masculinity is not just to walk home without fear, or if with fear of attack then to at least foresee victory. That masculinity is to make bank from one's doings, to capitalise and throw clout. That masculinity is a sly power play which has lost its old meaning.

5

In the past, for a living, I've washed dishes, scanned groceries, moved kegs, sold phones, slung pints, taught teens, made burritos, cleaned vomit, scooped dairy, packed boxes, tamped coffee grounds, picked orders; and invariably I completed these duties with the minimum passable effort. To none of them was I ever addicted, nor to any of them will I ever be. This much too is true—I do not dream of labour. I am no workaholic.

Nevertheless, without work, no Ward.

I arrived in Maynooth, I said, as something of a naive gurrier, and while my gullibility was founded on a number of assumptions—the largest being that in County Kildare I would meet like-minded people—it was especially radical for me to think that in Maynooth, unlike in Westmeath, I'd have no problem finding a part-time job that wasn't farming.

Hailing from a mid-earning household, I was ineligible for the grant that many students avail of, particularly those from my part of the country, which gives them the luxury of not having to work while they're in college. My father being a solicitor and mother a baker, there was never a chance I'd get it. Still, the parents sorted my tuition—said the rest was up to me.

I alighted in Maynooth with a fortnight's rent paid and a grand to my name, most of which by the end of September was gone. I'd precipitately bought a small library of books, non-essential to my studies, and would survive in October only if I budgeted scrupulously. I was too proud to call home for any kind of financial assistance.

To Dunnes, Tesco, O'Briens I handed out CVs, asking nose-ringed employees if I could speak to their managers. Most common was the wan glabrous man in a stained pinstripe shirt, his paunch slight yet protrusive, and how he'd stammer that the roster, eh, was... a- a- already full... full to the gills, so it is... of both part-timers and students.

I comported myself to pubs, restaurants, chippers; to petrol stations, phone providers, laundromats. All an exercise in futility. I had no contacts nor entry points: no uncles nor cousins to help get a foot in the door. And so long as I knew no one, unemployed I'd remain.

Then at Maebh Kealy's for pre-drinks, some chap said I was gorgeous and I offered, in all seriousness, to go down on him for fifty beans. He considered, or at least appeared to, and said matter-of-factly that there might be an opening at Brewhouse, where he worked, over near Brady's.

The following week I was serving lattés and paninis at what I thought was an appalling standard. The owners assured me that my skills were up to scratch.

Fast-forward a month later and I was supplementing my insufficient, part-time wages with paid shags across campus. This kind of work I got ahead in through Sean, my Brewhouse colleague, and a guy that he knew. Cormac didn't look or act like a pimp, but clearly that's what he was. The service was used mostly by dudes who had a fetish for payment, with soliciting services. We ate meals and we rode. Overall it wasn't bad. And because of my height I thankfully never felt threatened. In most cases, anyway, my clients were known about town. Or at least prominent on Grindr.

After Christmas I found work elsewhere, at Lev's Ice Cream Kiosk in Manor Mills. My amicable parting with Cormac wasn't what I expected. I had wanted, for my condition, a heated fight and a death threat and a constant living-in-fear: something to prove that my illness had cracks, that the full use of my feelings I would one day recover, that December wasn't a fluke.

December, naturally, containing my encounter with Ward.

6

Shortly after I started prostituting my body, I began to take refuge in non-binary politics and androgynous identities, and though my thoughts were amorphous, my writing even more so, I was comforted by the idea that something was there, in androgyny, on which the death of capitalism could potentially play out.

May I be safe.

The progenitor of these thoughts was my fractious mental state, whose wellbeing was deteriorating because of the nixer I was involved in. My simplistic theory was that in order to aid the recovery of unhealthy minds—for example, my own—we must remove from society all kinds of toxic work, and then eradicate all ties between work and gender.

May I be happy.

I was more numb than ever, and routinely questioned my sense of self. Not because I was sucking dick for money but because I was earning so little. A real man, I thought, would spread his cheeks and earn enough to last two or three weeks, rather than three days.

May I be healthy.

I hated these thoughts, hated myself more for them. I didn't want to be a man anymore.

May I live with ease.

To escape was the only solution. Not to move forward with my problems but to leave each of them behind.

7

'There has been much talk of late,' a Word doc of mine from that period reads, 'about a masculinity in crisis, about conservative models of masculinity crumbling under modern theories of gender. In this instance, the heteronormative male experiences a deterioration of power and, consequently, becomes angry. He is undone by the strong independent woman, or the proud homosexual man, and he has no choice but to pine for an age in which labour was separated according to gender, in which bravery, chest-bumping, and intrepid flights of fancy were integral to the act of being a man.

'If this type of masculinity is set to topple— provided we're saying it hasn't done so already—it follows that a new or modified gender construction ought to take its place: a feminine-masculine hybrid which I would like to call a socialist androgyny.'

This I tried to tell Ward, in Brady's in December, on a Tuesday when it was quiet, while most students finished the last of their semester essays. I wasn't one yet for the solitary pint that I am now, but dropped in regardless after shutting Brewhouse for the night. At the bar there was Ward, sultry, gaunt. I didn't notice him till I'd ordered my Guinness, waiting the accustomed hour for her to settle and the bartender to top her up. Ward was reading *Solace*, by Belinda McKeon, which fortunately I had read not that long ago.

'Oh, *Solace!*' I enthused, in introduction. I neglected to add that I hated reading in bars.

With that there followed a discussion of contemporary Irish feminism and, eventually, a confusing debate about how best to debunk gender norms in today's political climate. Ward said my idea for a socialist androgyny, while cute, was incoherent and untenable.

He drank everything. Stout, cider, lager, red ale, IPA, whiskey, Sambuca, gin. He never had the same beverage twice. I on the other hand remained faithful to my Guinness, and the only thing more copious than our alcohol consumption were the laughs we gladly basked in. I never brought up his wink. At the mention of Wardian conditioning, though, he went red. His deranged means of prompting conversation I told him I found intriguing. This partly sobered up our mirth and nudged our spiel in a different direction.

As we trudged out of the pub, pulling towards his apartment, I worried that my bellyful of hops would prevent me not from getting hard, but from reaching orgasm—and being an intractable bastard, I would keep fucking or tugging until I had brought myself to come; or until I collapsed, prostrate, defeated, conceding the alcohol had won.

I needn't have worried. Ward was so far gone after his melange of drinks that, even as a bottom, he lasted only a minute before he excused himself to get sick.

I gave serious thoughts to fleeing. In the past I deserted hook-ups with the impunity of an infant. But in the face of Ward's impotence, and in light of his violent retches, I found myself considering how he would feel if I ran away. Lately I had been reciting a version of the Metta prayer during situations of distress, for both myself and others. I was trying to cultivate my intuitive sense of empathy, which had been in hibernation for years. Thus with Ward's security and pleasure, health and ease, on my mind, I chose not to leave but to brew tea.

Mine was golden and strong, Ward's not yet complete. On a plastic tray: a two-litre jug of Avonmore skimmed milk and, beside it, a steel bowl of sugar. I would have pinched a packet of biscuits had his cupboards not been so scant. On entering his room this time I noticed it was clustered with trinkets and LED lights. On the walls loomed posters of WWII novels. I hadn't known anyone to ever enframe the work of Graham Greene.

He spoke mostly about his dissatisfaction with how his PhD was playing out, his recurring nightmare about the fate of his thesis. In it, his supervisor conversed with a future postgraduate, retrieving from a high shelf a decade-old book whose grimy leather cover he blew and wiped clean. The destiny of his thesis, he feared, was for it to become unsolicited dust on his supervisor's shelf.

'I'd be shocked,' he said, wobbling, his tea spurting out of his I Heart Plymouth mug, 'if I manage to put it to bed by the end of the summer. Positively flabbergasted.' This despite, in our first seminar, he said he'd finish it by April.

We never did quite say goodbye. After I jammed on my shoes and hobbled past his chipped green door, he drunkenly likened the gist of his argument—again, a lot to take in—to that album by Bowie, you know, the drug one.

'Yeah,' I said, gesturing, 'fucking... *Station to Station.*'

'Yeah!'

I nodded. 'Cool...'

We waved so long in silence. I hadn't mentioned my work, or what we might do about *us*. My short walk home was cold but, for the most part, I didn't notice—I was too preoccupied wondering how someone in Ward's position got that far up the academic ladder and pronounced Bowie as *bough-ee*.

This complicated how I felt about him overall.

8

During Ward's tutorial debut there were three blood-splashed copybooks, one broken nose, two phlegm-ridden heads, four horrified onlookers—who subsequently chose another minor—and, on the whole, a torrential shower of verbal abuse.

It died down on its own, with Ward staying seated the whole time. Maebh's words on Wordsworthian masculinity gave us an opportunity to reappraise what had just happened; those who had thrown punches and hocked spits were all male. No one could say they were satisfied with how the tutorial had played out. There had been no victories. Everyone had lost.

'I think, uh...' Ward said nervously, as the appropriate time came for us to all part, 'that we might keep this among ourselves, no? There's no need, not *really* anyway, to get someone of higher authority involved, is there?'

Outside the warm autumn air rustled.

'Let's have a show of hands. If you would like to press charges, to get the rest of the university involved, and to prevent me from potentially getting my PhD, please raise your hand.'

Many scowled, frowned, simmered. But none raised a hand.

'Excellent. And for those who would like to come here on Thursday, forgetting that this foolish affair ever transpired, and to try out a decisively ordinary means by which to tackle literary criticism—that is, through plain old pleasant conversation—let's see your mitts in the air.'

His was the first to go up. The rest followed, albeit ruefully.

'Marvellous,' he exhaled, relieved. 'Truly marvellous.'

Ward made good on his word. The tutorials became uneventful, their content routine. The same three spoke, same guy was late, same girl failed to print off her readings. It was just that: uniform, disciplined, grey, the same.

Most didn't learn about Ward's disappearance until after Christmas. It marked a first for the university. No member of its faculty or student body ever vanished before. A distinct and foul mood hovered over that January's exams.

In February a mass took place in the university cathedral, at which his parents were present. Andrew was meant to meet them on Christmas Eve at Birmingham Airport, where Andrew's father, Jonathan, waited wearing a suit, a shiny cap, and a solemn glare. At the arrival gate he held up a sheet of paper on which, in bold 72-point Georgia, stood the words: *Andrew Ward, PhDunce*. An hour passed before he and his wife Kay began to worry.

*

134

When I question my ability as an academic, I see Ward in his carrel, in his igloo of Mann books, contending with similar issues. When I go days without speaking to anyone other than my supervisor, I picture Ward ordering a twelve-year-old Red Breast whiskey, I imagine his I Heart Plymouth mug. And while the attendant feeling is uncanny I can't say that it's love. Rather, it's like gratitude but weirder. A warped appreciation for my current life circumstances. He taught me to roll with my problems, to be thankful for my headaches. To stop looking for solutions—or diversions—without entirely giving up. All by making me feel heard.

'That's sweet,' he said that night, taking a deep slurp of his Heino. 'But what's the selling point? If masculinity's about power and capital, what's the benefit of this… socialist androgyny? Why not a female hierarchy? Why, indeed, not a matriarchy?'

In his long spectral face I discerned the point I'd been chasing for months.

'It's just Voltaire for millennials,' I slurred before composing myself. 'That's all there is to it. Old ideas, anew. You level the playing field to give everyone an equal chance. Make do with your lot and simply cultivate your turf.'

Outside we shared the last of his Carroll's; an odd choice for an Englishman. Between drinks, we admitted, we patched up a number of holes in the ceilings of our lives. For the minute it was dry and the warmth would linger until the next rains fell.

We both knew they were never really that far away.

THUMBNAILS

BY SHANNON YEE

I have tried desperately, repeatedly, not to write
about you, but I loop back in the same way she and I
looped around and around and around the roundabout
surrounding the Arc de Triomphe, not knowing how to
get off once we'd gotten on, the thrill of the ride turning
into momentary panic and back again.

You return in early morning. You surprise me with
your tenacity. This time, it's your hands. They surprise
me with their tenacity, their fumbling figuring out.
With you, there's only forward, in front of, 'yes, and',
tomorrow—but not necessarily forever, and I have to
remind myself of that when it feels we're on repeat,
making me loopy with the looping, dizzy with the
time-diving, as I look around me, furtively, secretly, only
occasionally, for an exit sign overhead.
The way you sleep still gets me. You're transported back to
a months-old you. Arms above your head is a sign of full-
slumbered surrender as I try to ease out the door. You stir.
I stop. You settle. I've never held my breath for so long.

*

When we—she and I—took that photo of your two-day-old toes gripping her tummy, I knew our family would be one of repeated disclosure, of outdated paperwork, of deep-breath decisions couched in firm smiles. We—she and I—hoped the recurring reveal would be less intimidating as we travelled the X-axis of time with our Y-axis of experience. We expected you would make up stories about a Daddy who lived in New York, Hong Kong, and London (on rotation), but we never imagined the most frequently assumption of us would be that she was your Granny (my mother?!), how off so many's radar our family would be.

For your first time in the cinema, we carefully chose a movie with a female lead who looked like you with almond-shaped eyes, strong hair, courage, and a love of baòzi so you too would be confident enough to guide a magic Pixar fur-flecked yeti home to Mount Everest. At the end you shouted out, 'He's home with his mommies!' and I cried in the dark at your logic's purity.

When we—she and I—took that photo of you on your first day of school, I wanted to tell you to let me know *immediately* if there was any hint of the heteronormative family as the only kind portrayed in your classroom. I had prepared for the 'Family Tree' school unit since your birth with books about a variety of families, mostly from the animal kingdom (chinstrap penguins and Laysan Albatrosses were somehow more acceptable than two grown women). We had quizzed the Principal about how Mother's and Father's Days were handled, and explored what options were available for Religious

Education, because I'd be damned if you would be made audience to a public lecture about how our family is wrong. I wanted to tell you I was poised with the school's anti-bullying policy, the United Nations Convention on the Rights of the Child citations, the drafted email to the Minister of Education, and a Human Rights barrister on speed dial. But I didn't.

I didn't because your Barbies (I know) married each other in their townhouse and had hundreds of kids and you once pretended to give birth to a baby bunny who cried and after a moment's rest, you announced you had to head back to the office 'to go to work'. Little did you know how much you knew.

When we—she and I—took that photo of you at the beach (that monumental summer when a pandemic made us into a pressure cooker), what started as stress-filled coaxing you into neoprene and sand wreaking havoc on your smooth soles' senses, gradually evolved into endless hours of you tempting waves, racing them to the shore with glee-filled shrieks and victorious taunts. It was there we learned you would come to it, all of it, in your own time (so exhale). It was there you learned there are times you have to turn your back to remain standing.

When we—she and I—took the photo of the first meal you made for us—her and me, your face beamed with pride over the ham and cheese sandwich and your fine motor skills. I watched you line up the knife along your index finger to thumb, then cut off the crusts because that was an expression of love in culinary. I wanted to tell you it wasn't your role to take care of either of us, of anyone but yourself, for we were doing our best to figure out a way to live (not forever) just for long enough.

When we—she and I—took that photo of you and your friends (the first you chose to frame), I wanted to tell you we knew your mini-skirt and heels were hidden in a bag in a bush around the corner. We knew that the contents of our limited liquor cabinet had been siphoned off until the bottles held mainly tap water (we were playing the long game). I wanted to tell you that, like at soft play spaces in toddlerhood, you must always keep sight of your friends and stick together (I did), wanted to tell you I wanted to know (but didn't really) the extent of the danger you circled, enticed, and ingested. I wanted to tell you that friendship was as much about finding, figuring out, letting go and landing in another loop.

We were still grappling with how to step aside just enough.

When we as a three are public, we—she and I—check ourselves first for the risk for you, for us, split second calculating if what is gained in visibility outweighs what could be lost in a moment of insult. I could be brave for me, and braver for you (she was always the bravest and boldest). We modelled pride and head held high, but the problem with oppression is it primes you for rejection. It is the kind of fulfilment that surprises you, always, with its sting.

When we—she and I—took that photo of you on your first (double) date and you were scowling so hard it cracked to reveal your glee underneath, I wanted to tell you what consent looks like, sounds like, feels like and when you lose your virginity it's never what you think it's going to be. But I didn't. I couldn't. To do that would have to also be ready to answer questions about how our—her and my—sex life worked in the context of puberty and pregnancy and, monumentally, how you came to be.

I wanted to tell you that both boys and girls will break your heart at its different stages of growing and scarring and strengthening, that sometimes the girls are worse because you'll probably have swapped clothes and been naked in front of each other at some point before you were ready. But always, always, the first heartbreak is the worst. It may haunt you, but it will heal you and I promise you'll be ready for the world again, fuller from the loving and losing.

I wanted to tell you that we—she and I—were intellectually prepared for adolescent rebellion and parental rejection but we weren't ready for the way we fought hard, fought fierce, for you and our three would be the same way you would fight with us. Hurling genetics (mine) and eye color (Mama's) at us, saying you 'never asked for a family like ours,' almost as strongly as the intense emotions that overtook you. Though we were to be unconditional and unwavering, in those moments we frantically searched through our shards of heart-sore for strength to quietly supply to you, like the pack of tissues, a fiver and our phone numbers we slip into your coat pocket (just in case).

We had the privilege of your ugly. You had the burden of ours.

When we—she and I—took that photo with you at the (final) final boarding call at the airport gate, we had just played Thumbwars to decide who would go to the shop one last time for the extra pack of gum, bottle of water, tissues, hand sanitizer and protein bar (that you wouldn't eat) for your long haul flight, and who would get one last moment of alone with you in person. I wondered about your return, wanted to ask you, but I didn't, couldn't, shouldn't. I wanted to tell you it was in similar early morning moments of embarking that she and I began looping together. There were many sunrises after sunsets that laid our foundation. There was that time we convinced ourselves we were sober enough to cycle down the middle of 4th Street on a bicycle together, fell over in front of a taxi in its iconic NYC yellow, clamboured ourselves to upright and stumbled through the West Village sidewalks to the apartment she was housesitting to wake up the next morning, holding hands towards brunch when a stranger stopped us and told us how in love we were. There was new and novel and 'never before have I'. There was a word we created for us—her and I— as 'l love you' didn't capture it fully it enough.

And it was in that first summer in the city of her and my twenties that you were born in our hearts (plural) and together (singular), hoping that one day the way we played 'someday' would come to stay.

I wanted to tell you (I wanted to) about traumas and tears we'd carried and weathered. There were egos and impatience and exhaustion, there was betrayal and rebuilding and steadfastness. There was a therapist who intertwined her hands to make a nest and told us that was where you lay. Still.

I wanted to tell you the things that really matter are to always carry a toothbrush and photo ID in your bag, that the three most important things you can say are 'Thank you', 'I'm listening' and 'I'm sorry' (but not necessarily in that order), that our nagging is love poorly translated and that all the grey hairs on my, our—her and my—wrinkled bodies (my tits now as pert as two flat tires) are signs of our utter devotion to you, to we, to us as a three, to all you should be able to be.

Instead:

The glint in your eye and the love of craic is Mama. Your tendency to make lists and mistake excitement for anxiety is me. The serene pleasure from a single scoop of Honeycomb you 'make smooth' atop a cone is Mama. A pile of favourite pens stashed somewhere is me. The freedom unleashed from an impromptu contemporary dance duet in our kitchen is Mama, but when you 'feel the music in your heart', that's all you. A game of chasies before bedtime and a morning family cuddle is us-three-ours.

Don't erase one of us in your stories about home. Rage

about the casualties of menopause (first Mama's, then mine), menstruation (yours), and the carnage when they intersect, but balance them with your memories of snuggling into Mama's bosom, finding quiet on our laps, or absent-minding my earring'd earlobe between your thumb and finger.

Lead with love and integrity. Look someone in the eye when you say 'thank you'. Make friends with the cleaners (you've been one). Tip heavy at the bar. If you invite someone to meet, pay for the coffee (and if it's a mentor, it's lunch). Being empathetic and kind doesn't mean being stepped on. Never let anyone treat you like less because you've always been more. On your wedding day, have someone keep you on schedule. And if you're making history, open the day up to corsage-wearing supporters and circus performers. They will outnumber the bigots and carry your black taxi through the crowds to safety on a wave of love; the press can wait, for a day like that is more than yours alone.

So as I try desperately not to write about you, you are all that I can write about, with that way that you were born in our hearts (plural), poured into yours (singular), in the high hopes that you will loop back (in multiple), to us. What's working in our favour is the universal pull of the soil you're birthed on for there's something about this ancient Irish motherland, with its stories in song, sodden hills, and sideways-standing sheep that brought your Mama back, with me, and now, since you, prevents me from leaving.

143

BIOGRAPHICAL NOTES & ACKNOWLEDGEMENTS

John Boyne was born in Dublin, Ireland, and studied English Literature at Trinity College, Dublin, and Creative Writing at the University of East Anglia, Norwich.

He has published twelve novels for adults, a short story collection and six novels for younger readers, including *The Boy In The Striped Pyjamas*, which was a *New York Times* no.1 Bestseller and was adapted for a feature film, a play, a ballet and an opera, selling around ten million copies worldwide. Among his most popular books are *The Heart's Invisible Furies*, *A Ladder to the Sky* and *My Brother's Name is Jessica*.

He is also a regular book reviewer for *The Irish Times*. In 2012, he was awarded the Hennessy Literary 'Hall of Fame' Award for his body of work. He has won three Irish Book Awards, and many international literary awards, including the Que Leer Award for Novel of the Year in Spain and the Gustav Heinemann Peace Prize in Germany. In 2015, he was awarded an Honorary Doctorate of Letters from the University of East Anglia. His novels are published in over 50 languages.

His latest novel, *A Traveller at the Gates of Wisdom*, was published in July 2020.

Araby was previously published in *Dubliners 100*, an anthology from Tramp Press (2019).

Emma Donoghue, born in Dublin in 1969, is an award-winning novelist, playwright and screenwriter, living in Canada with her family. Her novel *The Pull of the Stars* became a bestseller in the US (*New York Times*), Canada, Ireland and Britain on publication in July 2020. Set in Dublin during the Great Flu pandemic in 1918, it is about a nurse midwife, a doctor and a volunteer helper living through three days in a maternity quarantine ward. A bestseller in Canada and Ireland, *Akin* (2019) is her first contemporary novel for adults since *Room*. It follows a retired chemistry professor and his eleven-year-old great-nephew from New York on their journey to the French Riviera to unearth his mother's wartime secrets. *Room* was shortlisted for the Man Booker and Orange Prizes and has sold over two million copies. She adapted the novel into her first feature film, *Room*, directed by Lenny Abrahamson, which was nominated for four Academy Awards for Best Adapted Screenplay, Best Director, Best Picture, and Best Actress (won by Brie Larson).

Her other books are the historical novels *The Wonder*, *Frog Music*, *The Sealed Letter*, *Life Mask*, *Slammerkin*, and contemporary ones *Landing*, *Hood* and *Stir-fry*; two family stories for younger readers illustrated by Caroline Hadilaksono, *The Lotterys Plus One* and *The Lotterys More Or Less*; short-story collections *Astray*, *Three and a Half Deaths* (UK ebook), *Touchy Subjects*, *The Woman Who Gave Birth to Rabbits*, and *Kissing the Witch*. She has also published literary history including *Inseparable*, *We Are Michael Field*, and *Passions Between Women*, as well as two anthologies that span the seventeenth to the twentieth centuries.

Mary Dorcey is a critically acclaimed fiction writer and poet. Her work is taught and researched in universities from North America to Europe, China and Africa.
She won the Rooney Prize for Irish Literature in 1990 for her Short Story collection *A Noise from the Woodshed*. She has published nine books, three of fiction and six of poetry. Her New and Selected Poems, *To Air the Soul Throw All the Windows Wide*, was published in 2017 by Salmon Poetry. Her novel *Biography of Desire* (1998) was a bestseller and has achieved widespread critical acclaim. She was the first woman in Irish history to campaign publicly for LGBT rights and the first to address the subject unequivocally in literature.
A lifelong feminist and gay rights activist, she was a founder member of 'The Movement for Sexual Liberation' 1973, 'Irishwomen United' 1974 and 'Women for Radical Change' 1974. She is a Research Associate at Trinity College Dublin where for seven years she led seminars on Women's Literature and led creative writing workshops.
She is currently editing new poems for her forthcoming collection with Salmon Poetry.
She is completing a new novel, volume one of a duology, *A Dangerous Love*.
She was elected to the Irish Academy of distinguished writers and artists 'Aosdána' in 2010.

Neil Hegarty grew up in Derry. His novels include *The Jewel*, and *Inch Levels*, which was shortlisted for the Kerry Group novel of the year award in 2017. Non-fiction titles include *Frost: That Was the Life That Was*, a biography of David Frost, and *The Secret History of our Streets*, which charts the history of twentieth-century London. Neil's short fiction and creative non-fiction have been published in *The Stinging Fly*, the *Dublin Review*, *The Tangerine*, and elsewhere. He lives in Dublin.

James Hudson is a writer living in Dublin who enjoys using speculative fiction to explore perceptions of the queer body. His essay "Wanna See My Party Trick? *Stops Taking T*" appears in Monstrous Regiment's *So Hormonal* anthology, and he is the co-curator of a forthcoming collection of art and writing by LGBT+ young people with Pop Up Projects. He is also a librarian at the Small Trans Library Dublin, working to improve the accessibility of queer literature to trans people in Ireland.

Emer Lyons is a lesbian writer from West Cork currently living in Dunedin, New Zealand in the last weeks of a creative/critical PhD on shame in lesbian poetry. Her critical and creative work has been published worldwide in *The Stinging Fly*, *Poetry Ireland Review*, *Into the Void*, *The Cardiff Review*, and *takahē*. She has been shortlisted for the Bridport poetry prize, longlisted for the Fish poetry prize, and the Munster Literature Centre's Fool for Poetry chapbook competition. Her play *The Green* was nominated for the 2019 Dunedin Theatre Awards.

Jamie O'Connell's debut novel, *Diving for Pearls*, will be published by Doubleday in May 2021. To date, his work has been Highly Commended by the Costa Short Story Award and the An Post Irish Book Award Writing (i.e. Short Story of the Year). He has been longlisted for BBC Radio 4 Opening Lines Short Story Competition and shortlisted for the Maeve Binchy Travel Award and the Sky Arts Futures Fund. His short fiction has been published in a number of journals, featured on TV3, RTÉ Radio and BBC Radio, and he has read at many festivals and universities in Ireland, China, Spain and the USA. He has received bursaries from The Arts Council of Ireland, Culture Ireland, Cork City Council and Dublin City Council.

Colm Tóibín is the author of nine novels, including *The Master* and *Brooklyn*, and two collections of stories. His play *The Testament of Mary* was nominated for a Tony Award for Best Play. He is a contributing editor at the *London Review of Books* and Chancellor of the University of Liverpool.

Sleep was previously published in the print edition of *The New Yorker* (March 23, 2015).

Declan Toohey is from County Kildare. His work has appeared in *Soft Punk*, *The Dublin Review of Books*, *The Stockholm Review of Literature*, and *Stone of Madness Press*, among other outlets. He is currently based in Halifax, Nova Scotia, where he is at work on his first novel.

Shannon Yee (Sickels) is an award-winning writer. Her perspectives as an immigrant, biracial person who has experienced racism, and queer artist-parent with a disability living in post-conflict Northern Ireland are deeply embedded in her work. She is passionate about highlighting marginalized stories and their intersections to broaden the narratives being told (www.s-yee.co.uk). She has been fortunate to secure a number of grants and awards for her work, including the ACNI Major Individual Artist Award (2017) and Wellcome Trust Public Engagement Award (2012). Her self-produced play, *Reassembled, Slightly Askew* (www.reassembled. co.uk) has toured internationally since 2015 across Northern Ireland, England, Canada, Dublin and Hong Kong. It uses binaural sonic arts technology to immerse audiences in her autobiographical experience of nearly dying and subsequent acquired brain injury. Shannon is working on her first collection of short stories, courtesy of an ACNI grant. Her short story, 'The Brightening Up Side', published in *Belfast Stories* (Doire Press, 2019), addresses new motherhood, racism and tenacity in North Belfast. Her essay, 'Tectonic Plates and Pressure Cookers' (British Council NI, 2020) was published in the *Lives Entwined IV* collection. Shannon is also an LGBTQ+ activist. In 2007, she co-founded and co-produced OUTBURST!, the largest LGBTQ+ multidisciplinary arts festival in the island of Ireland. In 2005 she and her partner (Grainne Close) were the first public civil partnership in the UK. In 2017, they and the first male couple (Chris and Henry Flanagan-Kane) began legal action to bring same-sex marriage to Northern Ireland.

Editor: **Paul McVeigh**

Paul's debut novel, *The Good Son*, won The Polari First Novel Prize and The McCrea Literary Award and was shortlisted for many others including the Prix du Roman Cezam in France.

Paul began his writing career as a playwright in Belfast before moving to London to write comedy. His short stories have been read on BBC Radio 3, 4 & 5 and on Sky Arts. They have appeared in print in journals such as *The Stinging Fly*, and numerous anthologies including Faber's *Being Various: New Irish Short Stories* and *The Art of the Glimpse*.

He is associate director of Word Factory, 'the UK's national organisation for excellence in the short story' (*The Guardian*), and he co-founded the London Short Story Festival. Paul reviews and interviews authors, such as Booker winners Anna Burns and George Saunders, for *The Irish Times*, and his work has been translated into seven languages.

He was co-editor of the *Belfast Stories* anthology and was fiction editor at *Southword Journal*. He edited *The 32: An Anthology of Irish Working Class Writers*, out July 2021, which includes new work by Kevin Barry, Roddy Doyle and Lisa McInerney.